In a Heartbeat

MARKUS HARWOOD-JONES

JAMES LORIMER & COMPANY LTD., PUBLISHERS
TORONTO

James Lorimer & Company Ltd., Publishers acknowledges funding support
from the Ontario Arts Council (OAC), an agency of the Government
of Ontario. We acknowledge the support of the Canada Council for the
Arts, which last year invested $153 million to bring the arts to Canadians
throughout the country. This project has been made possible in part by the
Government of Canada and with the support of Ontario Creates.

Cover design: Tyler Cleroux
Cover image: Shutterstock

Library and Archives Canada Cataloguing in Publication (Paperback)

Title: In a heartbeat / Markus Harwood-Jones.
Names: Harwood-Jones, Markus, 1991- author.
Series: RealLove.
Description: Series statement: Real love
Identifiers: Canadiana (print) 20210205903 | Canadiana (ebook) 20210205946
    | ISBN 9781459416277 (softcover) | ISBN 9781459416284 (EPUB)
Classification: LCC PS8615.A7744 I5 2021 | DDC jC813/.6—dc23

Published by:
James Lorimer &
Company Ltd., Publishers
117 Peter Street, Suite 304
Toronto, ON, Canada
M5V 0M3
www.lorimer.ca

Distributed in Canada by:
Formac Lorimer Books
5502 Atlantic Street
Halifax, NS, Canada
B3H 1G4
www.formac.ca

Distributed in the US by:
Lerner Publisher Services
241 1st Ave. N.
Minneapolis, MN, USA
55401
www.lernerbooks.com

Printed and bound in Canada.
Manufactured by Friesens Corporation in Altona, Manitoba,
Canada in June 2021.
Job #277241

For Andrew, my heart.

01 Departures

THE CONVEYOR BELT has a squeaky spot. A whine every few turns. I sit at the edge of baggage pickup. A warbled announcement welcomes me to Kelowna International Airport. With furtive glances to the dark maw of the luggage track, I will my suitcase to appear and free me from luggage limbo.

"Luggage limbo . . ." I quietly repeat the phrase. There's a ring to it. My hands slip into the pocket of my sweater. I pull out a notebook and grab the worn pencil crammed into its folds. *Luggage limbo*, I scribble down. *Endless turnstile* . . .

"What rhymes with turnstile?" I mutter through my options, "All in a pile . . . Once in a while . . ." A squeal cuts through my concentration. I grit my teeth and glare as the baggage track whirs to life again. A family of sunburned faces huddles around, jostling for their suitcases. In my journal, I flip the page and start a new line: *Canada Goose jackets. Ski-goggle tans.*

At last, a heavy, neon-pink suitcase thuds into view. I gather up my things and weave through the crowd. I grip the bag's handle and don't need to check the tag. I know it says *Melanie Quan* — my mother's name, by marriage.

Mom always says she never figured herself as the type to settle down. Definitely never thought she'd change her name. Then she met Shana and "everything changed." Whatever that means. Just like that, Melanie McMartin became Melanie Quan. And when I was born, she became Mom and Shana became Ma. Seventeen years later, my name changed too.

Though, I don't think they saw that last one coming.

See, when I was thirteen, we had a guest speaker at school. He was supposed to teach us something about equality or how bullying is wrong . . . All I remember is that he mentioned being a "trans man." Before that, I'd never realized how much a couple words can change your whole world.

It took a while before I clued in anyone else on my big self-discovery. In the end, I came out by accident. I was just fiddling around with my Facebook profile — I never realized that a gender update would get auto-posted to my feed! All of a sudden, everyone was sending congratulations emojis and asking if I had a surgery fundraiser. Meanwhile, I was barely working myself up to buying a binder!

Thankfully, my mothers' only complaint was that I didn't tell them first. I thought for sure Mom would go on about my "betrayal of womanhood" or something cringey like that, but Ma must've talked her through all that second-wavey stuff *before* the family meeting. For my seventeenth birthday, the two of them even surprised me with a trip to Service Ontario. They'd done all the paperwork for my name change in advance. All I had to do was sign a form and wait for my new ID in the mail.

Darting through the airport, I press a hand to my pocket and feel the outline of my passport. My heart still flutters thinking of the name inscribed inside: *Lucien M. Quan*. That's me.

A breath of cool air rolls across my face. I pass through the airport doors and sunlight breaks, gold and warm against my skin. The parking lot is slick with melting puddles, memories of snow. I'd heard the winters were mild out west, but this is even better than I'd hoped. I peel off my coat. January here feels like springtime back home.

Toronto's a big city but growing up there makes it feel small. I've lived on the same street, in the same two-bedroom apartment, for as long as I can remember. At my alternative school, my accidental gender reveal was briefly big news to the hundred-person student body. I was never great at making friends, but suddenly everyone wanted to know me. I was bombarded with questions: How did I know? Was I having "the surgery"? What were my opinions on neopronouns or hormone blockers?

The attention was almost fun, if awkward. Then, the most popular kid in school came out too. They were so much more prepared, with easy answers to everyone's questions and a penchant for public speaking. Pretty soon, they'd started a Gay-Straight-Alliance and even won an award for championing gender-neutral washrooms. It didn't seem to matter that I'd asked for the same things when I was in grade nine, but back then everyone just thought I was being a "good ally."

I knew I couldn't spend one more semester in a school full of posers. I needed to get out, see the world — figure myself out on my own terms. Once I had my new passport, that urge to run only got stronger.

When I pitched the idea, Ma wasn't a fan. Apparently, "someone like me" shouldn't travel on my own. But Mom had my back. She told me she remembered the feeling — that drive. To go somewhere, *be* someone new. She said she knows what it's like having everyone think they already know all you can be.

With my parents more-or-less on board, there were still just two small problems: time and money. I had to finish high school *somewhere*. Plus, as much as my folks say we're "comfortable," I know we don't have the dollars to drop on an international trip. I figured that would be the end of it. Cool idea, can't afford it. Story of my life.

That's when Mom got a call from her sister, my aunt Jean. Turns out, she's got a daughter heading off to University of Toronto and is in need of a place to stay. Even better, Jean works as principal of a high school and could pull some strings to transfer me in. Next thing I knew, it was all arranged. Cousin Jeanette would stay in my room and I would get to spend a whole semester living in Vernon, British Columbia.

Standing at the airport entrance, I can't help but stare. Beyond the lines of parked cars and idling taxis, gigantic mounds of earth reach for the sky. They're flecked with brown and green, white peaks lined with glittering fir trees. I've never seen real mountains before.

Mom never talks about growing up in Vernon. All I know is, she left around my age and didn't look back. Meanwhile, the McMartins have never come for a visit or invited us for a holiday. Without a face to a name, I search the parking lot for a stranger who could be family. I wonder if Jean looks like Mom, all big curls and freckled cheeks.

A silver pickup catches my eye. Its engine roars like a beast. A Canada flag is plastered to the corner of its tinted windshield. Sunlight glints off its bumper and I wince, blinking back spots. When I get back my sight, the truck is bearing down towards me. A loud honk cuts through the parking lot. The air in my lungs is frozen. My legs feel like two blocks of cement. All I can think is that I'm fifteen minutes into my fresh start and about to get hate-crimed in the parking lot.

02 Motion Sickness

"HEY, LOU!" The truck rumbles to a stop. At the wheel is a young man not much older than myself. Nineteen, at most. Elbow resting out the window, he pulls at a scraggly, copper-coloured moustache. "That's you, isn't it? You seemed taller on Facebook."

A memory slowly pieces itself together. A profile picture of a boy in massive sunglasses, holding a large fish. At last, a name makes it out from the raw recesses of my throat. "Jer . . . Jerald?"

"Ha! Only Mom calls me that." A laugh bounces out of my cousin as he hops down from the truck. "Call me Jerry. Now come on, they're waiting on us for dinner." He grabs the suitcase from my hands and tosses it into the back. With no other option, I clamber around to the passenger side. Heart still pounding, my hands shake while buckling my seatbelt.

Jerry eyes me sideways. "Rough flight?"

"Something like that," I mumble.

With a shrug, he turns up the radio and pulls out of the parking lot.

"Hot food, coming through!" Jerry shoves past my chair, casserole hoisted above. "Make way, make way!" My waist is pinned against the heavy dining table.

Across from my seat, a rough copy-paste of Jerry eyes the steaming dish. "Mac 'n' bacon?" He smacks the table. "Shit, yeah!"

"Joey, mind your manners!" cries a voice from

the kitchen. Through a window in the wall, I can see the top of Aunt Jean's head bobbing back and forth. "And get your elbows off the table!"

Joey makes a face and slides back into his seat. Behind him, a tall man hovers in the archway between here and the living room. I don't know much about my uncle George, except that he's Jean's second husband and his bloodshot eyes have yet to waver from the hockey game playing out on their widescreen TV.

"Elbows in," he grumbles. "Keep it tight." I'm not sure if he's giving orders to his stepsons or his team. Maybe both.

Jerry finally sets down the pasta dish, right in front of my plate. Eyes darting to the kitchen, he snags a forkful of macaroni for himself. Yellow cheese strings across the tablecloth and lands on the front of his shirt.

"Hey, what the hell!" Joey whines, "Mom, did you see that?!"

"Language, Joey!" Jean hollers back. "Nobody likes a tattletale."

Jerry smiles with his mouth full and gives a playful

punch to his brother. Joey scowls and shoves him back. The two begin to tussle back and forth.

"Put him in a lock!" George cries out. "Come on, Ref! What're you thinking?"

Joey's hand smacks against the table. His plate flips, catapulting its cutlery. I duck past a spoon and it smacks into the wall behind me.

"Whoops!" Jerry gives a rough laugh. "Sorry about that, Lou!"

I bend down to collect the stray silverware. "Actually, it's Lucien . . ."

"All right, boys." Jean's voice moves into the dining room. "Settle down." When I sit up, she's setting down a platter of roasted chicken. Steam fogs up the glasses on her rosy, pink face. Her hair is lighter than Mom's, strawberry blonde with salt-and-pepper roots. "Now, let's start with some grace."

"Like, the Christian kind?" My mouth goes dry. The only prayers I have in my repertoire are the witchy chants I learned when Ma went through her pagan phase.

To my great relief, George stands up and smacks his stomach. "Rub-a-dub-dub, thanks for the grub!" He hollers, "Yay, God!" The whole table claps in unison, except for me. Jean adds in a quick amen.

"Ah . . . men," I follow suit, a half second too late.

The room becomes a whirlwind of flying elbows and jostling dishes. Hands reach across the table for salt, pepper, ketchup and mayo. Dodging the fray with the ease of an expert, Jean takes my plate and returns it to me, full. "Go ahead," she nods. "Dig in."

I stare down at a pile of orange pasta and pasty meat; iceberg lettuce drizzled in ranch and bacon bits. It's as if Aunt Jean decided to whip up everything that my gluten-avoidant, dairy-free, farmers-market-every-Sunday mothers would never make.

My stomach grumbles. I haven't eaten since Mom made me a spinach-banana-oat milk smoothie for breakfast. Looking around at the assortment before me, I chew on the inside of my cheek and ask, "Do you have any . . . vegan options?"

Joey laughs under his breath. "What kinda snowflake —"

"Shut up, dude." Jerry shoves at his brother, fighting back a smile.

"Hush!" Jean snaps at both of them. "Now, I'm so sorry, Lucien. It's just like your mother not to mention — are you lactose intolerant?"

I shrug. "Well, not exactly . . ."

"Allergic to milk, then?" Jean's already up and on her feet. "I think we have some extra salad without the dressing."

My mind screams, *I've been vegan since I was eight* and *milk gives me a wicked stomach-ache.* But my mouth says, "I'm sorry. It's fine."

"You sure?" Jean's face appears in the kitchen window. "I could whip you up some crackers and — well, something."

"Really, it's okay. Thanks." I grab my fork and stab it into a hunk of chicken. I try not to think too hard about the texture as I bite down, pulling apart the thin lines of muscle and fat. "This is all so great.

You didn't have to have a big dinner just for me."

Jean glides back to her seat and tucks a cloth napkin onto her lap. "Oh, it's no trouble," she says. "Family dinner is the most important part of every day."

"*Every* day?" I glance around the table.

Jerry's texting, phone barely concealed from view. Joey's busy ladling on another helping of macaroni. George pushes back in his chair, craning his neck towards the TV. "House rules," my uncle speaks from the side of his mouth. "Six o'clock or you don't eat."

A forkful of half-chewed meat sits in the bottom of my throat. My stomach is already starting to turn.

03 Passing Down

"SO, *LUCIEN.*" When Aunt Jean says my name, she grins like we're sharing a secret. Elbow-deep in the sink, she rinses each dinner plate. "First night in Vernon, new school on Monday — you must be so excited!"

"I guess." I take a soapy cup and place it in the dishwasher. "I don't really know what to expect. Mom hardly ever talks about growing up here."

Jean clucks her tongue. "That's no surprise." She holds a crusty fork up to the light. "When Mellie was your age, all she ever talked about was moving to the big city."

"Mellie?" I swallow back a giggle. "I never heard that nickname before."

"I told her, Toronto's too far." Jean takes a thin, yellow sponge from behind the tap. "Vancouver would've been better. Even Calgary or Winnipeg." She scrubs each tine of the fork until it sparkles. "We could see each other on holidays; make sure our kids know each other. But did she listen?"

". . . No?" My cautious answer is drowned out by noise from the next room over. Loud shouts, heavy boos. Sounds like whatever sports game is on, it's not going well.

Jean places the last dish into the rack and slaps the washer shut. "You sure you don't want to watch TV with the boys?"

"Um, I'd love to." I shuffle my socks on the kitchen tile. "But I'm pretty tired . . ."

"Of course." Jean dries her hands and leads me down the hall. "We've got a bed all made up for you."

Behind the farthest door, a narrow set of stairs leads downwards. With a tap on my shoulder, Jean steps down into the shadows below. I'm supposed to follow her but my feet don't seem to know that yet. A queasy feeling rises in my stomach. The stairs seem to stretch out forever.

"Lucien?" A voice calls out from the darkness. "You all right, honey?"

A troubling question bubbles to the top of my mind: How do I really know if this *is* my aunt Jean? How can I be certain any of these people are who they say they are? What if my real family is out there, looking for me, while I'm trapped in here with a bunch of strangers trying to lure me into their murder basement?! A dozen short films play inside my head, all of them ending with me chopped up in a thousand pieces. My mothers wouldn't even know to look for me until summer!

"Um . . ." Fists tight, I can feel the pulse of blood in my palms. I force myself down one step. The wood lets out a tiny scream. "I'm not sure . . ."

A hanging light bulb hums to life. "There we go." Jean stands, her hand on a pull-cord. She glances up at me and waves. "It's just down this way."

"Yep," I squeak. "Right behind you."

My socks soak up cold from the cement floor. The ceiling rumbles like a passing subway train, paired with muffled shouting. We must be under the living room. Jean leads the way through a maze of hanging plastic and pink insulation. "It can be a little tricky to get around down here," she tells me. "We're still finishing the basement."

"Is this where your daughter was living?" I ask.

Jean gives a hearty laugh. "Oh, no! But your cousin Joey's already got the second bed upstairs. And Jerry came back to us after he lost his job last week, so he's in Jeanette's room for now." She leads me around a corner to reveal a half-finished room. There's a sunken purple couch, a single lamp, and a thin rug stretched across the floor.

"Now, it can get a bit chilly at night," Jean tells me. "But don't worry. I found some extra blankets and brought down the space heater." She reaches behind the couch and plugs in a long, orange extension cord. "Of course, we could have doubled you up, upstairs. But I thought you'd like some privacy."

Past the pipes that run along the ceiling, I can still hear the medley of men shouting down their sports game.

"Right. Privacy, appreciated." I drag the corners of my mouth into a polite smile. "Thank you, Auntie. For letting me stay here."

"Oh, our pleasure!" Jean's rosy cheeks show dimples when she smiles. "You're a McMartin, after all."

"It's actually my middle name —" I start to tell her but something above us clatters and smashes.

"I better go make sure those boys aren't tearing the house down." Jean clicks her tongue and hurries back towards the stairs. "Let me know if you need anything!"

"Actually," I call after her, "I wouldn't mind —"

The door above clicks shut.

The fold-out couch whines when I sit. My suitcase is set at the end of the bed. On the nightstand, a small note lists the Wi-Fi password and curfew hours. In the far corner, the basement window rattles as a draft sneaks in along its edge. So much for that mountain view.

My phone's at one per cent. I pull out my charger and notebook, try to scribble down a few lines while my cell comes back to life. *Bedroom of doom ... Cavernous and cold* . . . After a few failed starts, I rip out the page and toss it aside. Nothing worth saving.

Once connected to the internet, my phone starts to buzz. Missed spam calls and delayed app updates. I curl under the blankets and swipe to Instagram, mindlessly scrolling past manicured selfies and highly staged animal photos. I try checking some stories, but it's all holiday vacation shots. Old classmates and friends of acquaintances, posing on sunny beaches or waving from ski lifts. Different people posting the same kind of stuff, over and over again.

The only posts that really catch my eye are from

the poetry and spoken-word artists that I follow. They're supposed to inspire me, but guilt bites at the back of my throat. How does this writing thing come so easy to them? Why do I even bother trying?

I'm about to shut off my phone when a new message pops up. It's the family group chat. They must've noticed I came back online.

Ma: You get there okay?

There's a pang in my chest. I fidget with the edges of my binding vest — maybe I shouldn't have worn it for the whole flight.

My phone buzzes again. Incoming photo. Mom crowds the camera while Ma's thumb covers the bottom corner.

Mom: Missing you already!

Ma: Send a pic so we know you're safe and sound?

With a sigh, I flip to the camera. But my background is all pink insulation. I try moving the frame, but now it's too dark. I consider inching closer to the window but the last thing I want is to come out from under these blankets.

I toss aside the phone and tell myself I'll text them back tomorrow.

Rolling over, I say a silent wish that the futon won't snap shut. With a wiggle, I slip out of my binder. Its worn Velcro pulls apart with ease. Eyes heavy, I let out a long breath and slip into an early sleep. My phone hums softly in the darkness behind me.

04 Hold On

I WAKE UP AT NOON to a wall of grey against the basement window. When I slip out the McMartins' back door, a layer of fresh snow covers everything in sight. All I hear is the sound of my own shoes as I crunch along the sidewalk.

The snow here is different, fluffy and light. Nothing like the street slush of Toronto. Only a few cars mosey along the road. I pass old Victorian houses, a churchyard woven with boot prints. Down the hill, a strip of shop windows and string lights. Sunlight breaks through the midday clouds. Vernon spills out like a picture on a postcard.

"A postcard . . ." I fish into my pocket, the plastic of my pen cool to the touch. I didn't think to bring gloves. Once on the page, the words seem so much less profound. I give a half-hearted attempt to find a rhyme. "Bank card . . . Avant-garde . . ."

Sometimes I wonder why I bother writing things down. My big ideas never seem to go anywhere. When I hear a catchy song or watch a clip of spoken word, it all seems so fluid. But my scribbled lines always come out clunky and dull. As I round the bottom of the hill, I wonder if I just need a change of pace. Could Vernon have the inspiration I've been looking for?

"Ah!" I cry out as my foot slips on a patch of ice. Arms flailing, my notebook and pen fly in opposite directions. In a second, I'll feel the smack of hard pavement. I see it all now — head cracked open, fresh blood on the snow. The flashing lights of an ambulance. The paramedic's face when my binder is revealed during CPR.

I brace for impact. But the sidewalk doesn't come. Instead, I smack into a warm chest. Strong hands catch my shoulders. Someone laughs. "Whoa, there!"

I look up and find golden eyes, hidden slightly in a cascade of silver bangs. A beautiful stranger holds me tight. "You okay?"

"No!" I stammer. "I mean. Yes. Thanks." My heart pounds in my ears. Pushing off, I brace against the closest building. "Sorry. I was just . . . on autopilot. Wasn't looking where I was going."

"Happens all the time." The boy shrugs, a guitar slung over his shoulder. "Especially with out-of-towners." The stranger snags my notebook from a nearby snow bank and hands it back to me. His face is youthful and round, a thin moustache along his upper lip.

"Thanks." I take my book back. "But, how'd you know I'm not from around here?"

"Cute ones never are." He winks and offers his hand. "I'm Alder."

"Lou — uh, Lucien." I stumble over my own name as I clasp his palm. My hands are so warm they're practically steaming. There's no way he doesn't notice.

"Lucien." He says my name with a smile. "Let me guess, wrapping up a ski season up at Silver Star?"

"Me?" I give an involuntary giggle, pull back my hand and pivot into a cough. "No, I'm not —"

"Ah, so you're a cottager then." Alder eyes me up and down. "From one of those families that rent cabins out on the mountain?" He nods towards the main street ahead. "I'd be happy to show you around, if this is your first time into town."

"Uh . . . Yeah." I pull at my jacket. "You got it. I've just been . . . cottaging it up. Up there." As soon as I say the words, the lie feels obvious. "I'm sorry," I tell him quickly. "I don't why I said that. I'm not actually a tourist."

"Good thing I'm not actually a tour guide, then." Alder tucks his arm under my elbow. His smile doesn't falter. "Now, let's get you somewhere warm."

IN A HEARTBEAT

"You must've have really pissed off someone in Toronto!" Alder laughs and kicks a pebble into the street. A couple of pedestrians glance in our direction.

My shoulders rise and I mumble into my coat, "It was kind of . . . my idea."

"Seriously?" Alder eyes me over with a slanted grin. "You moved across the country. On purpose. In the middle of the school year." He snorts. "That's a *choice*."

I brush aside the snowflakes that cling to my shoulders. "Okay, fine. Yes, it was kind of a big jump."

"Kind of?" Alder gives me a playful push and I can't help but smile back.

We pass along faded shop windows packed with knick-knacks and antiques, displays of self-help books and crystals. On the pavement, a rainbow sidewalk peeks through the afternoon traffic. The faded colours match peeling stickers plastered across several storefronts. The smell of fresh-baked bread drifts from a bakery across the street. My mouth starts to water. I pull at Alder's sleeve. "Let's go in there."

Alder crinkles his nose. "Way overpriced. I only go there at closing, when they sell off the day-olds. You can get five for a buck, if you haggle."

I pout but keep moving along, following Alder's long strides. Up ahead, the rich scent of fresh coffee pours from the open door of a café. The place even has a cute little bean mascot on its awning. This time, before I can even say a word, Alder shakes his head.

"That place is so pretentious. And the coffee sucks." He stares down the foggy windows as we pass. Inside, a woman at the counter gives a long look back. "Also," he mutters, "the barista and I have a . . . history."

I flash some side-eye. "Fine," I grumble. "I'll get a latte later, I guess."

At the next turn, there's a grocery market advertising a sale on "SuperFoods." A woman with ropey blonde hair pushes a full cart through the automatic doors, cloth bags packed to the brim. I shrug in the store's direction. "We could try and score some free samples?"

Alder gives a non-committal grunt. "Maybe some

other time. Watch out, though, if you end up shopping there. There's a big markup on anything organic."

"So, what?" I scowl. "Nothing here is actually worth visiting?"

Alder chuckles. "Not quite."

Outside the freshly waxed doors of a corner bank, there's a man huddled into a sleeping bag. Alder stops to drop a couple Toonies into his cup. "Good to see you, Frankie."

"You too, kiddo." The man cheers his cup in thanks. As we move along, he waves and calls, "Have a good day, ladies!"

My stomach drops. Less than a day here and I've already been clocked. But before I can say something, Alder waves back and whispers, "Don't mind the old guy. He can't see crap without his glasses."

The storm in my chest starts to calm. I clear my throat. "How do you know him, anyway?"

"Growing up here," says Alder, "you get to know just about everyone. If you take the time to stop and say hi."

Suddenly, we take a sharp turn. "Come on." Alder pulls me into a narrow alleyway. "We're almost there."

"Almost where?" I yank myself back and plant my sneakers in the melting snow. "Where are we going?"

Alder doesn't answer. Running a hand across the alley's crumbling brick, he traces faded layers of graffiti. A second later, he presses up against the wall and promptly disappears.

A draft runs up behind me, a chill along my spine. I scramble after him and find a door tucked into the brick. It's practically invisible when glanced from the street. Two words are etched across its yellowed glass: *Longbox Records.*

05 Other Side

WARM, MUSTY AIR washes across my face. I blink, eyes adjusting to the dim and dust-filled light. I'm faced with racks of records. Stacks on stacks of LPs and 45s that nearly reach the smoke-stained ceiling. The whole place smells like cigarettes and mothballs. It reminds me of the pop-up shops you'd find in some gentrifying corner of Toronto's west end. Except this seems like the real deal. Aloud, I wonder, "What is this place?"

Alder offers his hand. "A place in Vernon that's worth visiting."

His touch sends a shiver through me. Alder deftly dodges piles of records, pausing occasionally to point out a rare gem or funky cover art. Finally, we arrive in a clearing of folding chairs and a small stage propped up by milk cartons.

Alder sets down his guitar. "Give me a sec." He nods towards the back counter. "Talk to Sox if you want a drink or something."

Behind a counter, a clerk with a faded green mullet slouches from the record store's backroom, a milk crate of records in one hand, a yellowed paperback novel in the other. A peeling nametag provides an introduction: *Sox (they/them).*

I hover, waiting for Sox to notice me. Eventually, I give a quiet cough. They don't look up, but a pierced brow raises slightly. I take my chance to ask, "Uh, how much for a tea?"

Sox waves in the direction of a small electric kettle and several mason jars stuffed full of tea bags.

A cardboard sign tells me to *Pay What You Can, Take What You Need*.

The kettle boils, slow but steady. I sift through a collection of mugs and steep a cup of Earl Grey. When I dig into my jacket for change, a hand rests on my shoulder.

"Find what you need?" asks Alder. I blush and nod. "Hey, Sox. Add this one to my bill, eh? I'll get you back on Friday."

Sox flips a page of their book, not looking up. "That's what you said last week. You know the whole idea of a tab is to pay, eventually."

"You know I'm good for it!" Alder shrugs and leads me aside. Sox flips a lazy finger as we go.

Resting in a metal folding chair, I watch Alder tune his guitar. Droplets of Earl Grey drip down to nip at my fingers. Alder's acoustic-electric is covered in stickers for bands I've never heard of and various political causes. My stomach flutters as I notice one that reads: *Not Gay as in Happy but Queer as in Fuck You*.

He looks up at me. "So." Alder plucks a few strings. "What's your deal?"

"Me?" My face drops into my mug. "What makes you think I have a deal?"

"You really don't know how to relax, do you?" Alder laughs and starts to strum. A few chords resonate between us. "I just want to get to know you better. What do you do for fun?"

"Fun. Right." My tongue has gone numb. "I have fun."

"Yeah, you seem like a real party animal." Alder starts messing with the dials on his amp. "Not at all anxious-and-avoidant."

I sit up against the chair's cold metal back. "What's that supposed to mean?"

"Nothing, really." Studying his fingers, Alder works his way through a careful pattern. "I just was raised by a couple of shrinks, you know? Sometimes I pick up on things."

"What, you're saying you can read me?" I roll my eyes.

"Mm, I'd guess . . ." Alder's gaze flit back to me, just for a second. "Separation issues. Intrusive thoughts.

Maybe a tendency to freeze, fawn and flee?"

I sputter on a gulp of hot tea. "That's — I'm not —" Wiping a few spilled drops off my shirt, I start gathering my things. "Whatever. Thanks for the tour. I gotta head back, though."

Alder laughs under his breath. "Of course you do." He strums the guitar again and glances up. "Hold up. Are you actually leaving?"

Jacket clutched tight, I shrug. Alder sets down the guitar to hurry after me. "Look, I'm just talking shit," he says. "I'm sorry. For real."

I screw up my mouth, hoping for a cutting remark to surface. Instead, another voice shouts, "Alder, buddy!"

I glance back. A couple teens with middle parts and aviator glasses push into the shop. One of them waves a pair of drumsticks in the air. "What's up, man?"

"Ugh, these guys," Alder groans under his breath. He squeezes my shoulders. "Just give me a couple seconds, Lucien. Wait here?"

The heavy footsteps behind us make their way closer. "Fine," I mutter.

Alder plasters on a wide smile and hurries past, leaving a chill in his wake. "Dudes! I didn't think you'd get here so early." He greets his friends with elbow taps. I watch them push and joke with each other. Alder doesn't turn back, doesn't introduce me.

In a couple minutes, even more strangers roll into the tight space. The door's broken bell struggles to announce each new arrival. I'm faced with a wave of all obscure band T-shirts, washed-out jeans, stick-and-poke tattoos and septum piercings. Everyone seems to know Alder. Someone with freckles and blue-streaked hair rests a hand on his shoulder. My stomach turns.

I shrink back against the wall and pull out my phone. I've missed three calls. Text messages are waiting.

Joey: Mom's asking where you are.

Jerry: Coming back soon? Call if you need a ride.

Jean: Dinner's started. Come home now.

How is it almost six o'clock already? I look up and search for Alder. Should I say goodbye? I can't catch sight of him in the bustling crowd.

Maybe it's better this way. I drop my empty mug with Sox and skirt along the wall until I reach the exit. One hand on the door, I hear someone call my name. A flutter of excitement and relief twists up in my stomach when I turn and find Alder wading towards me. "You're heading out?" he asks. "For real?"

I bite my lip. "I was supposed to be home a while ago."

"Look . . ." He starts shuffling through his pockets. "About before, I didn't mean to put you on blast. I just want to get to know you. What actually matters to you, you know?"

"Words." My answer comes out so quick, I think it surprises us both. "Sorry. That's stupid."

"No, words are cool." Alder moves in a little closer. "I like words."

"Well, me too," I chuckle. "I guess that's obvious. I just mean, I think about them. A lot. Words I mean." My palms are so sweaty, I try to wipe them on my jeans. "Sometimes I write them down and . . ."

"Like, poetry?" Alder tilts his head. "You're a poet?"

I just shrug.

Someone calls Alder's name from the stage. He glances back for a second, then whispers, "Well, all right, then." He motions for my hand and I give it to him. With a marker from his pocket, Alder scrawls a note.

"What's that?" I ask.

"A souvenir," he tells me. "You did complete the tour, after all." He pulls back and reveals a smudge of seven digits across my palm, a phone number. Alder closes my fist and holds my gaze for a second longer. "Next time, let's talk words." With that, he's gone. Back to the stage.

I step out into the chilled evening air. The whole way back up the hill, my hand stays warm.

06 Sharkbait

I STARE AT THE WORKSHEET on my new-to-me school desk. Polynomials, linear relations — I know I've heard these words before but my mind won't put them together. It's my first day at North Valley Secondary and I'm already completely lost.

At the front of the classroom, Ms. Schmitke fiddles with the Smart Board. She's a young teacher, tall and slender with bright blonde hair. Her colourful scarf shimmers as she jumps from topic to topic. Apparently, today is mainly review. It all seems new to me. The teacher talks so fast, by the time I figure out how to ask a question, we're onto another topic.

At my school back home, math was more like music class. We'd build projects, do puzzles. If I got lost, I'd just ask someone how they were figuring it out. We always worked on the answers together. Here, the desks are lined up in sharp rows. Most of the other students look half-asleep — until Ms. Schmitke's sharp, blue eyes dart back from the board. That seems to be enough to make everyone sit up straight and at least pretend to listen.

Something flicks against the back of my head. A crumpled note falls to my feet. Its folded edges give hints at a crude character.

"Hey!" A broad-shouldered girl with short, frizzy hair wiggles in my direction. "New kid, pass it on!" I scoff under my breath and kick the note back in her direction. I might be new but I'm not going to get baited into being a delivery service.

I turn back towards the front and find

Ms. Schmitke's sharp eyes focused right on me. "Do you have something you'd like to share with the class, Lucien?" The whole room turns to look. I shrink back into my chair and shake my head. "I understand you are new here," the teacher flashes a tight smile. "But if we have something to dispose of, it should be put in the recycling."

My neck is stiff as frozen metal. "Sorry," I mutter and stoop for the note. With heavy feet, I carry the crumpled paper to a blue bin by the door.

"All right." Ms. Schmitke gives a loud clap. "We're all caught up on last semester. Now, please finish up your review sheets and turn them in at the end of class."

By the time I'm back in my seat, I'm surrounded by scribbling pencils. My own paper is marked only by sweaty fingerprints. What was I thinking, transferring in my final year? How am I supposed to get through a whole semester like this? Failing now could mess up my GPA, screw up any chance at university . . . Blood pounds in my ears while my mind does back flips through worst-case scenarios.

Ms. Schmitke weaves along the desks, hands clasped behind her back. When a student raises their hand, she pauses to offer whispered advice. My own arm is impossibly heavy. It takes everything in me to weakly lift it.

Something whistles over my head. A paper airplane heads for a brunette with a long braid that sits to my left. It loses altitude, skitters across the floor and stops right at Ms. Schmitke's heel. When she turns, I realize my hand is still raised.

"Lucien." Her perfect smile twitches. "What did we just talk about?"

"I'm sorry — I didn't —" I choke on my words. The teacher bends down to collect the note. From the corner of my eye, I spot that same girl folding yet another plane. I practically leap out of my desk to snatch it from her hands. When Ms. Schmitke turns back, she sees me standing, crumpled paper in hand.

"That's quite enough." Ms. Schmitke marches towards her desk and grabs her tablet. She scrolls, types something down and then sets her piercing gaze back on me. "Now, Lucien, would you like to explain to the class why you've chosen to disrupt our learning environment?"

"It wasn't me," I try to tell her.

She purses her lips. "All right. Would you like to inform us of the culprit?"

Everyone is staring. I'm surrounded by hungry eyes, waiting for more drama. The real note-passer pushes a finger to her lips. Finally, I answer, "I didn't see."

"Hm." Ms. Schmitke knits her blonde brows. "Lucien, hear me when I say, I understand how hard it can be to start over at a new school."

A wave of relief passes over me. "Yeah," I sigh, "it's actually —"

"*Please* allow me to finish," she snaps. Someone at the back of class lets out a giggle. "While I sympathize with your situation, my classroom is a place of equality and *respect*. Do I make myself clear?"

My stomach drops into my shoes. "I never —"

"Do I make myself clear, Lucien?" Ms. Schmitke repeats. "Or are we going to have a problem?"

My mouth goes dry. I have no idea if I'm supposed to answer or stay quiet.

The school buzzer breaks through, announcing the start of next period. My classmates fall into scattered conversation, zipping backpacks and shuffling feet. Ms. Schmitke gets caught up with another student. I manage to slip out with the crowd.

I'm a few paces down the hall when someone calls to me. "Hey, new kid!" The paper-airplane-maker swings an arm around my shoulder and tousles my hair. "That was way cool of you. Thanks for not ratting me out to Ms. Shit-key!"

I shove her off and pat down my bangs. "It's whatever."

With a shrug of my backpack, I start back down the hall. The girl follows at my heels. "The name's Maggie," she says. "Ms. S has kinda had it out for me since day one."

"Gee," I roll my eyes. "Wonder why."

Maggie spins around to walk backwards. "It's actually kind of sad. She's got this really rare condition. She can't feel any happiness or joy . . ."

From the corner of my eye, I study her face. "Seriously?"

"Dead serious." Maggie wipes a finger along her eyelid. "I just hope, one day, there's a surgeon brave enough . . . to extract that massive stick lodged up her ass!"

Maggie cracks herself up, backing right into another student. "There you are!" I recognize her, the brunette from class. "How many times have I told you? Stop trying to pass me notes."

"Aw, come on, Pippa." Maggie nudges my arm, like I'm in on the joke. "You know I was just messing around."

The second girl looks up and down the narrow hall. A handful of students linger by their classroom, one of the teachers is locking up his door. Pippa drops her voice and hisses, "Can't you just text me like a normal person?"

"But I'm *not* a normal person." Maggie wraps an arm around Pippa's waist. "Isn't that why you *like* me?"

Pippa's amber cheeks flush rose gold. She pushes up her round glasses and turns towards me. "I guess we both owe you one."

"Hell yeah!" Maggie wraps her beefy arm around me too and starts dragging us both along. "Come on, lunch is on me!"

07 Pull Up

IN CHATTERING CLUSTERS, students lean against lockers and prop themselves along the stairs. Bagged lunches are balanced on laps beside convenience-store hot dogs and clear bags of candy. The air is thick with the sweaty bodies of high schoolers all chowing down at once. Maggie and Pippa move through the chaos with ease.

"Home, sweet home!" Maggie plops down on a narrow bench shoved between two vending machines.

I look over my shoulder. "Don't you have a cafeteria?"

"Not anymore." Pippa lightly taps on Maggie's knee to open a seat. "They used to set up tables in the gym. Now they have basketball practice at lunch, so."

"Me and Pip have had our name on this spot since forever." Maggie smacks at the bench and makes a space for me to sit. "Close enough to the library to keep the jocks away, far enough from the music room so we don't have to listen to a capella rehearsals." She nods at the vending machines. "Plus, I'm pretty sure the school puts some kind of high-pitched noise source in these things to try to stop kids from loitering."

I take a step back, eyeing the machine.

"Don't believe a word Maggie says." Pippa pulls out a glass container filled with veggies and rice. "If anything, they're probably pumping extra sugar into the food so we all get addicted. Even though all those sugar crashes will likely lower the overall grade-point average."

Maggie snags a stalk of celery from Pippa's lunch. "That's capitalism for you," she says with a crunch.

"Sure . . ." I slide myself down to the furthest edge of the bench. In the depths of my bag, I find a take-out container packed with leftover macaroni and a baggie of soft carrots. I rub my stomach, nursing the indigestion to come.

"That looks amazing!" Maggie leans over. All I have to do is weakly wave it towards her and she eagerly accepts my lunch. Scooping up a forkful, she says, "You're kind of quiet, aren't you?"

"Um," is all I can think to answer.

"Lay off, Mag." Pippa selects some fried tofu squares from her lunchbox and passes them to me, along with a dollop of rice. "Lucien is probably just adjusting. I bet it's a real shock moving here from Toronto."

"How did you — ?" I start to ask.

"No such thing as a secret around here," Maggie cuts in. "So, like, do you know Peaches? Maybe Shawn Mendes?"

Pippa prods at Maggie's shoulder. "Don't be obtuse."

"Your butt's obtuse!" Maggie jabs back.

"Uh . . ." I briefly consider claiming my moms

are celebrity chefs or movie producers, that we've got a fancy house on the Bridle Path. After a couple seconds, I admit, "No, nobody like that. But, one time they filmed some of *Scott Pilgrim* on my street?" Maggie's eyebrows shoot up into her bangs and I fight back a smile. "Oh, and for a while I went to school with a kid whose dad works at the Rogers Centre. He got to meet Feist once. Apparently, she always asks for kale in her dressing room."

"I told you this guy was cool, Pip!" Maggie smacks a plastic container lid like a crashing cymbal. "Oh, sorry — you *are* a guy right?"

The smile on my face freezes into place. There's a sharp pinch in my nose like I have to sneeze.

Pippa groans, "Maggie, have some tact for once."

"Is it that obvious?" I whisper.

"Wait, are you actually?" Maggie wiggles in her seat. "Like, trans. For real?"

"What's the alternative?" laughs Pippa. "Trans for fake?" She adjusts her glasses and tells me, "Don't take Mags as a representative of the general population.

You're doing a great job, totally under the hetero-radar."

I glance between the two of them. "Wait, are you . . ."

"She is," Maggie nods. "I'm just her girlfriend."

"We can totally help you out," says Pippa. "I know the best doctor in town for puberty blockers — or estrogen, if you're feeling ready for that."

"And I got your back if anyone messes up your pronouns!" Maggie declares, louder than I'd like. "Oh! Do you have a girl name you want us to use?"

"Wait, no —" I blink back a dizzy feeling behind my eyes. "I'm not a trans girl . . ."

"Are you non-binary?" Pippa lights up. "I've been thinking of trying the they/them thing. Seems like a lot of work though."

"No, I'm a he/him." I shake my head. "Like, a trans guy."

"Shit, really?" Maggie whistles through her teeth. "You look good, dude. Never would've guessed."

"Maggie, you can't say that." Pippa prods her partner's shoulder. "Sorry about her, Lucien. She's just excited."

"I mean, me too," I shrug. "I honestly wasn't expecting to meet any other queers. Especially not so soon."

"The community is pretty small around here," Pippa admits. "But we know how to how find our own."

Maggie pulls out her phone. "Me and Pip have already dated about half the lesbians in our age bracket. So, if you want, we could introduce you to a couple of the bi girls from the Christian school . . ."

"No!" I answer, probably too quickly. "Thanks. I'm okay."

"Mags, jeez," Pippa hisses. "He might not even like girls!"

"Maybe he's got his eyes on someone already." Maggie flashes a wry grin. "Or long-distance lover, back in the T-O?"

While the two of them debate my love life, I sneak a glance at my phone.

Alder: Thinking of yr face. Got plans later?

The back of Maggie's head juts over my screen. "That your sweetheart, waiting for you back home?"

"Not that it's any of our business," says Pippa. Still, I catch her eyeing my phone.

"Actually . . ." I press the screen to my chest. "You said that you know most of the queers in town, right? Because this guy named Alder just asked me out and —"

"Alder?" Maggie snaps. "As in, Alder *Vankleek*?"

"Of course." Pippa stabs at her rice and veggies. "He sniffed you out quick."

Maggie prods at her girlfriend. "You gotta let it go, Pip. I'm over it." Twisting back towards me, she nods with enthusiasm. "You're only sticking around 'til grad, right? Alder's perfect for a springtime fling."

My stomach starts to tense up. "I don't know. He *is* pretty cute, but . . ."

"I don't see it," Pippa huffs.

"Shocking." Maggie sticks out her tongue. "I am shocked by this."

"Maybe it's not worth all the trouble." I shrug. "Trying to date while stealth seems like kind of a headache. And having *the talk* with some guy I just met . . . Well, that's not exactly appealing either."

Maggie gives a snort. "I don't think that'd be an issue with Alder."

Pippa sighs and cleans her glasses on her shirt. "True. I guess that's *one* point in his favour."

I glance between the two of them before turning my attention back to Alder's text. Is he waiting for a reply? My thumb hovers over the keypad. "I don't even know what I'd say."

"I can help with that!" Maggie tosses the emptied Tupperware into my hands and snatches up my phone. With a couple taps, she flips it back to me. A new message sits on the screen.

Lucien: Human Bean. 4 PM. 😗

"What's that mean?" I ask.

Maggie flashes a set of finger-guns in my direction. "It means, you've got a date. At the local gay café."

Pippa tucks back her hair. "I don't know if two queer baristas makes it a *gay café*."

In my hand, my phone hums. An incoming text.

Alder: It's a date 💞

08 Rendezvous

STEAM FROM an espresso machine eats away the letters of a chalkboard menu. Alder leans against the café's front counter. "Coffee, black."

Tight curls pulled into a bun, the barista taps the order into a tablet. "And for you?"

"Me?" I point at myself. Her tired eyes roll towards me. "Sorry. Tea with soy milk. If you have it. Please." I fumble with my pocket and stuff a handful of change into the tip jar. "Thanks."

The walls of the Human Bean Café are covered in tall paintings. Portraits of coffee beans with human faces. I feel their eyes follow us. Alder sits in a booth by the back and catches me staring at a scene of humanoid beans playing poker. "I actually know the artist who makes these," he tells me.

"Oh?" I eke out a polite smile. "They're very . . ."

"Horrifying?" He cracks up. "Absolutely monstrous?"

"Completely creepy!" I wheeze something close to a laugh.

Alder leans back, hands behind his head. "Yep. Basically a big parade through the uncanny valley."

"Ha, yeah," I answer. "Totally." I wait for my brain to think of something funny say in reply. Unfortunately for us both, nothing comes to mind.

Alder drums lightly on the table. I wipe my sweaty palms on my jeans. The inside of my head is like a frozen wasteland. Did I ever even have thoughts before this? Any hint of my wit or personality has become a long-forgotten dream. The silence between us is growing so big, I don't even know how to pierce it. Eventually, a desperate jumble of words fall out of me, all at once.

"Thanks for not ghosting me!" I wince and sit up against the hard plastic of the booth. "Not that I thought you would. Or, if you did, it would've been fine. Like, I wanted to see you. You didn't owe me anything."

"Yeah, sorry it took me a minute to text back." Alder studies his nail beds. "Been busy with the band."

"Uh . . ." I blink at him. "Your band?"

Alder brushes back his silver bangs. "Those guys from Longbox. We kinda jam together."

"Right." I try to smile but start to worry I'm showing too many teeth. How many teeth are people supposed to see, again? "Sorry I couldn't stick around to hear you play."

"You didn't miss much." Alder shrugs. "Honestly, we kinda suck. Our lead is such a total hot mess. Can't write lyrics to save his life."

"Could you . . . replace him?" I offer.

"I hope not!" Alder laughs. Am I supposed to join in? After a few seconds, he coughs and explains.

"Uh, because it's me. I play lead."

I fold back into the booth. "Oh. Sorry."

"It's all good." Alder slides his hand across the table, palm up. "We're still getting to know each other, right?"

I stare down at his hand. The longer I look at it, the further away it seems. "Speaking of . . ." I pinch my eyes shut. "There's something we should probably talk about."

"What's that?" asks Alder.

"Well, it's not like, a big deal or anything . . ." I chew the inside of my cheek. It's been a while since I had to put my whole gender thing into words. At least, with someone who didn't already know.

"No, I mean, what's *that*?" Alder points over my shoulder. I turn back and catch two sets of eyes. The peepers quickly duck from view.

"I told you not to look!" comes a whisper from the booth behind us.

"Shh!" another voice hisses. "They're gonna hear us."

Alder looks perplexed. "Do you know those people?"

I hide my face with one hand. "Never met them before in my life."

"Oh, Lucien!" Maggie pops up. "Hey, bud! Didn't see you there."

Pippa slips out beside her partner. "Wow. Yes. What a coincidence." She avoids my glare by adjusting her glasses. "And is that Alder with you — what're the odds?"

Alder raises his brows towards me. "Yeah. Real coincidence." Maggie and Pippa just linger there, at the edge of our booth. Alder nods towards the open seats. I shake my head no, but it's too late. He's already starting to offer, "Did you want to . . ."

"Join you?" Maggie jumps down beside Alder. "Hell yeah. Been forever since we hung out!"

"Has it?" Pippa hovers down beside me. "Feels like just yesterday that you and Mags —"

"Order up!" The barista swings by our booth. She passes Alder's coffee, fingers briefly brushing against his. "By the way, it's nice to see you. You're looking . . . good."

Alder's sunny cheeks start to flush. "Thanks." Once she's moved on to the next able, he explains, "We went to elementary together. Before . . . I switched to home school."

Pippa rolls her eyes. "Oh, here we go again with the home school." Meanwhile, Maggie takes the cream that came with Alder's coffee and knocks it back like a shot.

"Anyway." Alder blows aside the steam from his coffee. "I've been wanting to ask, how goes the words?"

"Oh! The words . . ." My hand goes to the notebook in my pocket. "Well, I dreamed up a couple lines when I was falling asleep last night. But I kinda forgot to write them down."

Pippa cracks a thin smile. "Been there."

I perk up. "You're a writer, too?"

"Yeah she is!" Maggie wipes off a milky moustache. "Pippa's on her way to being a mega-famous singer-slash-songwriter."

"Well, I don't know about that." Pippa pulls at the ends of her braid.

Maggie flashes a toothy smile. "I play backup, on piano. Plus, I do all the mixing. And the album art for Bandcamp."

"You always were a creative one." Alder's eyes sparkle in Maggie's direction. "Cool that you're in a band now."

"A *duo*." Pippa firmly sets down her tea in its saucer. "Anyway, it's just something we do for fun."

"Yeah, just fun. For now." Maggie snorts. "But after grad, we're taking this show on the road. Kelowna, Vancouver, Victoria . . . We're gonna be the next Tegan and Sara!"

"Except, not sisters?" I point out.

"Just as gay though." Maggie winks.

"Well, if you want a chance to try out your sound," says Alder, "I could talk to my buddies at Longbox . . ."

"Seriously?!" Maggie beams.

Pippa knocks her boot against my shin. I wince. I think that kick was intended for Maggie. "Thanks, Alder," she gives a tight smile. "But we're good."

"Come on, Pip," Maggie whines. "We're never gonna get discovered with like, three songs on the internet. We gotta get out there, get seen!" Maggie juts her chin at me. "You know what I'm talking about, right?"

"Me?" I freeze, one hand nursing my leg. "Um . . . Yeah. Totally." From the corner of my eye, I catch Pippa's death-glare. "But, uh, it's also really hard to put yourself out there. Can be a big transition . . ."

"Yes. Exactly." Pippa gives a curt nod. Maggie starts to whine again.

"Okay, guys." Alder sweeps his hands across the table. "Maybe you should take a breather . . ."

"Don't call us *guys*." Pippa's reply gets cut off. A sugar packet flies across the table and bursts against her shoulder. "What the — seriously, Margaret?!"

"Ooh, full name!" Maggie snickers, readying another packet in her teaspoon catapult. "Am I in trouble?"

"Oh, my god!" Pippa pushes back, jostling the table as she stands. "You're so immature!"

"I'm immature?!" Maggie snorts. "What about you — when are you gonna grow up and deal with your stage fright, or whatever?"

"There's probably a better time for this . . ." Alder tries again but no one is listening to his half-hearted couple's counselling.

"Okay," I announce. "Maybe we should all just go pay our bills . . ." I try to get up but my jacket is pinned behind Pippa's back. I twist upwards but my elbow bumps against Alder's coffee. In what feels like slow motion, the mug tips, splashes across his chest, then falls to the floor with a loud crack.

"Ah, shit!" Alder shouts, hot coffee dripping down to his jeans.

"What the hell, dude?!" Maggie snaps at me, snagging a handful of napkins.

Pippa waves down the barista. "Can we get a cloth over here?"

I stutter out an apology. The whole café is staring at us. I can even feel the coffee-bean portraits turn their eyes on me.

I grab my bag and make a break for it. Through the café door, a blast of cold bites my cheeks. My eyes start to water, stomach swimming. Every bottled feeling from tonight hits me all at once and none of them are good.

09 Call It Off

I PUSH MY SPOON around a mound of brown meat and boiled vegetables. Conversation among the McMartin dinner table has been fully fixated on some local hockey game. I don't try to follow the details. It's too confusing when you don't know the players . . . or the teams . . . or the sport.

"Hawkner handled that deflection." Joey spears his mashed potatoes. "They should've had the game in the bag!"

"Never would've happened without their goalie pulled," says Jerry. His knee rests against the table until Jean shoots over a stern look. His chair instantly drops back down.

"All with Spinowski on the bench." George gravely shakes his head. "What's the point in rolling lines if you're not going to make it through the series?"

I have no idea if they're arguing or agreeing. Under the table, I slip a peek at my phone. New texts from Maggie and Pippa have been coming in steady since our catastrophic double date. Meanwhile, the one person in Vernon I actually want to talk to has yet to reach out. Not that I blame him.

I flip to our last message. Alder confirming our date with that little emoji. My heart burns like it's fallen into my stomach acid.

"Lucien." I sit up straight. Jean's eyes are on me, her mouth a tight smile. "You know the rules. No phones at the table."

"Yeah, Lou," says Joey. Jerry snickers too. With a single look from their mother, both boys clam up quick.

"Now," Jean wipes her hands on a paper napkin. "I know we're all worked up about the Juniors' second round."

"Yeah," I mumble. "All of us, definitely."

"But that's no reason for poor manners at dinner." Jean starts to clear the table. "Why don't you all head over to the living room and watch the replay?"

"Now there's an idea!" George grabs his soda can off the table. "Come on, boys. They're doing a hall-of-famers special tonight."

"No can do." Jerry slips his dish onto Jean's growing stack. "I gotta meet up with Sarah Whittinger. She's got her sweet nineteenth this weekend, out at her folks' cabin in Lumby. And she said she needs *my* help to make it happen."

"I thought you only had a sweet sixteen?" I point out.

"Yeah, she *needs* you." Joey laughs and tosses a balled-up napkin in his brother's direction. "Or at least the keys to your truck. And your ID at the LC."

"Shut up, dude." Jerry shoves back his seat. "You'll see at the party on Saturday. She's totally into me."

"Saturday?" Uncle George furrows his brow. "But what about the game?"

"I'll still watch it with you, hun." Jean gives her husband's shoulder a squeeze on her way to the kitchen. "Let the boys have their fun." Jerry and Joey share a grin. "Oh," Jean calls over her shoulder, "and be sure to take your cousin!"

My cousins and I share a look of horror. Jerry starts to protest, "I don't know if that's such a good idea . . ."

"Nonsense." Jean appears in the kitchen window. I hear the tap squeak on as she fills the sink. "It'll be a great chance for Lucien to see more of the Okanagan. Maybe he'll make some new friends."

"Come on, Mom!" Joey whines. "Saturdays are for the boys!"

"All the more reason then!" Jean hollers over the clattering of dishes. "Not to mention, this way I know you'll be responsible and get home at a reasonable hour." She flashes a stern look towards both her sons. "Are we agreed?"

In a chorus of grumbles, Joey and Jerry slip from the table and head to the living room. George follows suit. While they settle in, I snag the last dishes from the table and head to the kitchen. When I find Jean, she's shaking detergent into the dishwasher. She asks, "Don't you want to go watch TV with your uncle?"

"Maybe in a bit." I lean against the counter and, out of habit, pull out my phone. There's a voice memo from my mothers, cancelling our call this evening. Apparently, they signed up for a 'yoga and yogurt' night. There's another message and something else catches my attention. It looks like I have an outgoing text . . . to Alder?

Jean tilts her head towards me. "Is everything okay?"

"Mhm, mhm." I answer through pursed lips, rapidly swiping my screen. This can't be real. Why would I send this? And when?!

Lucien: H

My mouth goes dry. I must have accidentally pocket-texted him during dinner. My first thought is to delete it, but it's too late. He's seen it. And now, he's typing a reply.

Alder: . . .

Alder: Sup

I blink down at the glowing screen. "What the hell is that supposed to mean?"

"Lucien, language!" Jean snaps the dishwasher shut.

I mutter an apology and speed walk out into the hall. Nose pressed to my phone, I nearly crash into an oncoming cousin. "Coming through!" Jerry grabs my shoulder and pushes me aside. "Sorry, little dude. Gotta go warm up the truck for Sarah."

"Yep. Totally." I start to shuffle past but Jerry holds on to my shoulder.

"Hey, hold up a second," he whispers with a look towards the kitchen. "So what's the verdict? Did you manage to talk her out of it?"

"Who?" I glance up, phone pressed to my chest. "Oh, right. The whole party thing." I slip from his grasp and scurry towards the basement stairs. "Don't worry. There's no way I'm going out to the middle of nowhere with a bunch of random dude-bros." As soon as I say the words, I try to choke them back down. "No offence to the bros, of course! It's not that I don't want to hang but —"

Jerry flips me a thumbs-up. "It's all good, little dude." He walks backwards down the hall. "No offence taken."

10 Letting Go

MY LUNCH is day-old meatloaf and a Ziploc of boiled peas. I crouch under the back staircase of North Valley Secondary, prodding at the leftovers. Above, I can hear a handful of the school's hockey bros shouting at each other. I'm not sure if they're fighting for fun or fury. I guess, maybe both. Down the hall drifts the sound of the a capella club struggling through a rendition of "Bohemian Rhapsody."

My notebook sits balanced on one knee. I tap my

pen against a blank page. *Stairwell of purgatory.* I scribble down the words. *An inferno of echoes . . .*

"So this is where you've been hiding!" Maggie pokes her head over the railing, a wicked grin plastered on her cheeks. I press the open notebook to my chest. There's a loud slam as the bros above start up another wrestling match. The choir next door cracks into the fandango.

Pippa steps down after Maggie. "You really picked the worst spot in the whole school to have lunch." She gives a long grimace. "What are you, a masochist?"

"Not that there's anything wrong with that." Maggie snorts. "We don't wanna yuck your yum." She extends an arm towards me. "But seriously, let's go grab our usual spot before someone steals it."

"Yeah, right." I sink back against the wall. "Look, it sucks enough being the new kid. Can't you two find someone else to torment?"

"Torment?" Pippa slips under Maggie's arm. She crouches beside me. "What makes you think we're trying to do that?"

"You can drop the act." I roll my eyes. "I know you were just hazing me or whatever. Making me think we're friends just to mess with me."

Pippa scrunches up her face. She looks back at Maggie. "I told you we shouldn't have crashed their date."

"You're the one who wanted to spy on them in the first place." Maggie shrugs her offered hand back into her pocket. "Look, dude, we're sorry. We weren't trying to mess with you, honest."

"But if it wasn't an act . . ." I study my shoes. "What about that big fight you were having?"

Pippa settles down next to me on the grungy tile floor. "What about it?"

"I don't know." I shrug. "It seemed kinda serious. Aren't you still upset at each other . . . or me?"

"Oh, that." Maggie leans back on her heels. "It's no big. One stupid fight doesn't mean we have to break up."

My teeth clench tight against my cheek. ". . . Really?"

Pippa tilts her head. "Is that how things went at your school — one rough day and it's just 'see you never'?" I shrug in response. She gives a brief sigh. "Well, we do things a bit different. There's not enough queers around here for that kind of burn rate."

"Yeah!" Maggie chimes in. "After like, six months, you'd run out of people to talk to. Now hurry up. Today, lunch is on me!" With that, she leans back against the stairway's double doors and slips into the hall.

Pippa shakes her head and calls after her girlfriend, "You say that every day!"

I linger on the floor, my legs still stiff. "So that's it?" I ask. "We're all friends again, just like that?"

"Just like that." Pippa opens a hand towards me. I take it and let her pull me up.

"Check it out!" Maggie smacks all the buttons along the vending machine. "I saw this online. If you know the code people use to stock these things, you can get stuff for free!"

Pippa pulls out a small blue lunchbox. "Don't you think it's more likely they just use a key?"

"Yeah right," Maggie snorts. "Would TikTok lie to me?"

"Oh, sweet Maggie." Pippa pulls out a palm-sized orange and offers half to me. "Did you even try to look up the codes?"

"Didn't have to." Maggie swipes over the keypad again, this time starting from the bottom. "Law of averages says, if I hit every possible combination, I'll get it eventually."

I fight back a laugh and tell her, "I don't actually think that's how the law of averages works." Pippa giggles with me. Maggie sticks out her tongue.

I bite into the orange slice. It's sweet, fresher than I expected. Reminds me of the ones Ma used to give me when I was getting sick. She always says Vitamin C can cure just about anything. The memory brings with it a gnawing feeling in my stomach. I suddenly wish I could just curl up in bed — my real bed, not that lumpy basement mattress.

There's a loud thud as Maggie punches at the side of the machine. I make a face and mutter to Pippa, "Do you think that's part of the life hack?"

"I doubt it." Pippa adjusts her glasses and gets up from the bench. "Here, let me help. You need to at least get a formula going . . ."

"Margaret Cooper." Brisk heels click towards us from down the hall. "And Penelope Little." Aunt Jean appears, sporting a sharp grey pantsuit and a stern look in her eye. "Why am I not surprised?"

The sweetness on my tongue turns sour, an acidic pang in the back of my throat. Maggie shoves her hands into her pockets. "Sup?"

"Hi, Principal McMartin." Pippa gives a too-sweet smile. "Didn't see you there."

"Indeed." Jean speaks through a tight frown. There's a faint twitch along her lip when she spies me on the bench. "Lucien? What are you —" She coughs and straightens her blazer. "Do you care to explain why your *friends* here are damaging school property?"

"Oh, Maggie was just . . ." The girlfriends glance towards me, desperation in their eyes. "Trying to get my change back?"

"That's right!" Pippa hops forward. "Lucien lost a whole four dollars in there!"

"Yeah!" Maggie chimes in. "We were just trying to help our buddy. Honest, Ms. M!"

Jean sucks air through her teeth, eyes darting between all three of us. "All right," she says at last. "Still, you can't go shaking that thing. It's a hazard." She digs into her pockets to pull out a ten-dollar bill. "Just go to the gas station next door. Get yourself a snack."

Maggie's hand darts out and grabs the cash. "Will do!" She snags Pippa as she hurries towards the school doors.

I step after them and whisper, "Thanks, Auntie."

Jean's expression softens, only slightly. "I've got a call in my office," she grumbles. With that, she clicks away as quickly as she came.

11 Rearview

MOUNTAINS STRETCH in long shadows on either side of the highway. My cousins make idle chatter in the front of the truck, their faces briefly lit by the headlights of passing cars. I sink down into the back cab half seat, furiously texting.

Lucien: I cant believe you talked me into this

Maggie: i can't believe u were srsly gonna skip out 😌

Maggie: sarah throws the most badass parties in the whole Okanagan

Pippa: her birthdays are pretty legendary.

Lucien: wish you two could have at least come with

Maggie: hard same.

Maggie: its cool tho, were doing date night

Pippa: *we're 😊

My phone hums as a photo comes through. A slanted shot of Maggie and Pippa, chowing down on a pizza with extra cheese and extra-extra pineapples. In the back, *But I'm a Cheerleader* plays on a laptop.

Lucien: omg jealous 😫😫😫 that looks like so much more fun

Pippa: it definitely is lol

Pippa: on a scale of 1 to 10, how awks is that car ride rn?

I eye the front seats. Jerry is grumbling about how they're going to be late, saying Sarah's relying on them. Joey just keeps making gross jokes and poking at his brother while he tries to drive. I brace myself, ready to run off the road at any second. Somehow, Jerry keeps us steady as we take an off ramp.

Lucien: I'm gonna say 99/10 for awkward 😣

Lucien: still, not as bad as when Jean kept trying to take photos of us all getting ready

Pippa: how do cis-het guys even prep for a party? 😬

Pippa: coat themselves in a toxic level of body spray? crease their basketball shorts?

Maggie: hey, i wear basketball shorts!

Pippa: we know ••

I laugh and try to text back, but the message doesn't send. My reception flickers down to one bar. Shoving the phone into my pocket, I look out the window and watch as daylight sinks from the sky. The truck turns onto a side road, then a street puckered with potholes, then a gravel path lined with fir trees. Low-hanging branches graze the roof as tiny rocks pop against the bottom of the truck like raindrops of a growing storm.

Nestled in the darkened forest is a tall, wood-panelled house. It pulses with music. Shadows pass across foggy windows. We pull into a circle of pickups and SUVs and Joey pulls a six pack from under his seat. "Bro, this is gonna be epic."

Jerry cuts the engine and looks over his shoulder. "All good back there, Lou?"

"Me?" My voice cracks. I force a cough. "Yeah, no, super good."

"You're in for the night of your life, little guy." Joey breaks loose one of the beers and tosses it back to me. I catch the warm can in my chest.

"You can't just give him beer!" Jerry shoves his brother. "He's like, thirteen!"

I scrunch up my face at the rearview mirror. "Seventeen," I tell them and pop the tab. The drink tastes terrible, but I force myself to gulp it down.

"Right on!" Joey gives me a high five and hops out of the truck. Jerry hesitates for a second, then follows.

I push down the front seat and clamber out into the night. It's warm, for winter, but a chill still runs down my spine. The so-called cabin is bigger and more extravagant than any house I've ever visited in Toronto. A handful of smokers wave hi to my cousins from the wrap-around porch. I catch a couple chuckles, whispers and nods in my direction. My face goes hot. I take another swig of warm beer.

Before he locks up, Jerry pulls a flannel shirt from the truck and tosses it to me. It's wrinkled, crusty and clearly too big around my shoulders. I wear it anyway and he gives an approving thump on my back. "Just try to have fun," he whispers. "And don't go too wild."

The cabin's air is warm and sticky. Music comes from everywhere. Sweaty teenagers shuffle around on some kind of chaotic circuit. A small group is playing darts, next to another bunch singing karaoke to a flat-screen TV. By the time I'm through the bottleneck of the entrance, I've lost all sight of Joey. By the stairs, Jerry's passing off a crate of beer. He's chatting with a girl, all smiles as she presses a hand to his chest. She's got a plastic tiara that sparkles when she laughs.

There's a rush of cold as the door opens behind me. More people push their way inside and I'm shoved deeper into the crowd. I duck under waving arms and bumping shoulders, side-step a splash of beer. Finally,

I surface in the kitchen. Marble counters topped with bowls of wet chips and stacks of solo cups. At least it's quieter in here.

I shove myself in a small spot next to the fridge to catch my breath. My head aches already. I chug the last of my drink and pull out my phone. At least my bars are back. I go to text Maggie and Pippa but . . . how do I even describe this place?

A handful of teen girls sit clustered around the kitchen's centre island. "So, story time!" One with a high ponytail sips her clear, fizzy drink. "I was in the bathroom, about to cut my bangs when —"

"One sec, Jess." Another lifts a finger and glares in my direction. "Um, are you seriously taking pictures of us right now?"

"What?!" I jump and nearly drop my phone. "No, of course not . . . I mean, sorry. I was just . . ." I latch onto the closest thing I can find — the handle of the fridge. I whip it open and grab the first thing I see — more beer. "Getting a drink!"

"Whatever," she huffs. "Creeper."

As I scurry away, I catch a whisper. "What a weird guy."

"Was it even a guy?" asks another. The whole group breaks into giggles.

I slip out the back door. The night air nips at my ears. A few partygoers gather around a growing bonfire. "Hey, buddy!" Joey appears and swings an arm over my shoulder, boozy breath in my face. He ushers me over to a group of guys. "Boys, this is my little cousin. Lou, these are the boys!"

"It's *Lucien*," I grumble. A few guys nod to me before going back to their conversation. I pretend to listen to their idle chatter while sipping on my second beer. It tastes a little better cold.

The bonfire is beautiful. Dancing blue flames cast shadows across the yard. Above, thin grey clouds part to reveal a waxing moon. Joey shouts and takes a running leap, just barely clearing the fire. I join with the crowd, laughing as he lands in cold mud. He yelps and pats down a stray spark on his jeans. I help jeer him on for an encore.

The stranger next to me elbows his friend. "Okay, what about her?"

"Hmm." The other guy leans over, eyeing a girl across the yard. "I'd say, three, seven. B plus."

"More like two, five, C minus," the first chuckles.

I fidget with the tab on my beer. My thoughts are going fuzzy. "What're you doing?" I ask.

The first guy scratches the patchy beard along his neck. "It's just guy talk."

I take sip of my beer. "I'm a guy."

The second dude chugs the last of his drink and tosses aside the empty can. "The first number rates a girl's top half," he tells me. "Second's their bottom. Letter grade for their face." He points to a young woman who's just stepped outside for a smoke. "Her? Four, two, solid B."

"That's my girlfriend, you ass!" the other man laughs. There's a rustling among the circle as they debate the first guy's assessment.

I blink a few times. The fire has turned all blurry. "Don't you think that's kind of . . ." I close my eyes to remember the word. "Degrading?"

Patch-beard scoffs and crosses his arms. "Don't take it so seriously."

"We're just having fun," says the other. "It's not like it means anything." He hocks a wad of spit.

I want to say more but the words are backed up in my throat. Instead, I down the last of my beer and walk away. One of them mutters after me, "How old is that kid, anyway?"

"Hey, Joey!" someone hollers. "How'd you get stuck babysitting?"

My cousin just laughs and runs at the bonfire again.

12 Slip Away

THE PARTY IS even louder than I remember. The kitchen has turned into a dance floor.

My mouth is dry. I squeeze to the fridge but there's only beer inside. The girl with the ponytail sits perched on a countertop. I wave for her attention. "Is there anything else to drink?"

She furrows her brows. "What?"

I force my voice louder. "Is there anything else to drink?!"

"I think they're using it right now." She points at some teenagers who've plugged up the kitchen sink. They're playing some kind of bob-for-apples drinking game. "Try the bathroom?"

"Not a sink." I mime a cup in one hand. "A drink!"

"In the basement, I think?" She shrugs and starts typing on her phone. That seems to be the last answer I'm going to get. I head towards the stairs.

The basement is all shiny leather couches and white carpet. Creepy, taxidermied animal heads hang on the walls. The room is packed and people are cheering. A short young woman scrunches up her face and bounces a small ball across a glass coffee table. It lands in a red cup and the room erupts in applause. The woman's opponent downs the drink, fizzy brown liquid spilling down his cheeks. I side-step the chaos, back pressed against a closed door. The handle is unlocked. I slip inside.

The floor is cool, white tile. There are racks of summer clothes, fancy sandals and wide-brim hats. Next to the walk-in closet, there's a washer and dryer along with an old fridge. I swing it open, hoping for water. It holds only rows and rows of pop.

I smack my lips and notice something tucked in the back. A clear bottle with a faded label. "Dr. McGillicuddy's Original Formula," I read aloud. Propped against the washer, I twist open the orange cap. It smells like peaches dunked into rubbing alcohol. "Ugh. Nasty."

I fish out my phone and flip to the group chat with Maggie and Pippa.

Lucien: I think I might literally be hiding in a closet 😂

Lucien: Is this the hetero agenda?

"Anybody seen my cousin?" A question floats from the other side of the door. "Short guy, kinda awkward? I'm supposed to get him home soon."

"Oh, yeah, I met the little guy," says another. "I think he's out back."

"Thanks, dude." Jerry's voice drifts away again.

I scowl down at the bottle in my hands. My wrists look so delicate in the heavy sleeves of my cousin's shirt. I roll them up and take a swig of that Original Formula. Instantly, I double over in a coughing fit.

After a few more sips, my throat is so raw I hardly feel the burn anymore. There's no word from Maggie or Pippa. I flip instead to that mysterious message from Alder.

"Sup. Su-uh-p. Souuuup." I crack myself up. "I should call him and just say that — souuuup!"

A tiny voice from the back of my mind screams that this is a bad idea. I wash it down with another swig, then smack the call button.

"Hello?" Alder's voice crackles through my phone speaker. "Lucien, is that you?"

There's a loud cheer from the next room. A millisecond later, it comes through Alder's side too. I blink a few times and look around the storage room. "Are you . . . here?"

"Where is 'here'?" Alder shouts through static. "Where are you?!"

I stare at the washing machine, watching the floor tilt sideways. "Laundry."

A moment later, the door to my hiding place swings open. Alder stands there, phone pressed to one ear. I stumble towards him and slip on the linoleum. Alder catches me before I face plant. "We really need to stop meeting like this." He grips my shoulders and sets me back up. "You feeling all right?"

"Yes. Definitely. Absolutely." I lean back on my heels. The wall behind Alder's head spins like a globe. From the open door comes a wave of shouts and boos. "Ugh," I groan. "Are they still playing beer pong?"

"I think they switched to flip cup." Alder flashes his sideways smile, "Why, you wanna play?"

"Absolutely not." I pinch my eyes shut. That only makes the spinning worse. "I think I need to get out of here."

"Understood." In one smooth motion, Alder guides me out of the basement, through the upstairs, out the front door. The fresh night air washes over me. I can breathe again.

When I remember to open my eyes, Alder's still standing there. All I can think to ask is, "What're you doing here?"

"I could ask you the same thing," he smirks. I just stand there, wavering slightly. After a beat, he shrugs. "Sarah and I are old pals. Believe it or not, I was at her sweet thirteenth. An all-night D&D party!" He looks back at the rocking cabin. "Funny how things change."

A wave of nausea rolls over me. It's like I've got a time bomb ticking in my stomach.

"There you are!" There's a slap on my back and I nearly keel over. Jerry's arm is on my shoulder. How long has he been there? "Dude," he says to Alder, "where do you think you're going with my cousin?"

"It's all right." I weakly wave. "We know each other."

"Good to see you, Jerald." Alder brushes aside his silver bangs.

"Oh." Jerry's eyes go wide. "Wow. I didn't even recognize you, A . . ."

"Alder." He offers his hand and Jerry takes it. They stand there, palms clasped, hardly moving.

"You look . . . good," Jerry says at last.

"Same to you," says Alder with a wink.

"Jer!" A woman's voice calls out from the porch. "What's going on out there? We need you to open this keg!"

Alder gives a pinky wave and sings, "Hi, Sarah!"

Jerry glances to the cabin, to me and finally to Alder. "Sure you can get him back to my place, safely?"

"I haven't been drinking, if that's what you mean." Alder shrugs. "Same address as always?"

Jerry just clenches his jaw and squeezes my shoulder. "You cool with this, little guy?"

I open my mouth to say, *don't call me little*. Instead, the bomb in my stomach goes off. Before I can even think, it's up my throat, out my mouth and all over Jerry's shoes. He leaps back and curses. I clutch my stomach. My lips and nose are burning. But at least that terrible, tilting feeling has stopped.

Alder pats my back. "Oh, city kids. How's about we get you home?"

13 Moon Meets Sun

COLD GLASS IS pressed flat against my cheek. I open my eyes to a dark highway. Constellations of small towns, rural homes, roadside gas stations. The car window is fogged with my breath. I peel myself up, wipe off a trail of drool on my chin.

Alder sits beside me. Two hands on the wheel, eyes fixed on the road. There's a slow, warming feeling underneath me. For a second, I panic. I can't have been that drunk, right? As if reading my mind, Alder points to a small light on the dash. "Heated seats."

I open my mouth to say thanks. The second I inhale, a wicked cough runs up my throat. My tongue burns with a distinctly peachy aftertaste. I double over, nausea catching up with me. "Who even *is* Dr. McGillicuddy?" I ask and wince at the dashboard clock. "And how is it already one in the morning?"

Alder taps open the glove compartment. An unopened water bottle falls onto my lap. "Hydrate," he instructs me. "There's a Clif bar in there too, if you're hungry."

"I don't know if I'll ever be hungry again," I groan. "Thanks, though."

"Anytime," says Alder.

The two of us settle into silence. We cruise through a housing development, past a strip mall with buzzing neon signs. I blink and we're pulling up in front of the McMartin house. The living room lights are still on.

There's a sinking feeling in my gut. The truth tumbles out before I can sugar coat it. "I don't want to go in there."

Alder shrugs. "You don't have to."

I lean into the soft leather of my seat. "What am I going to do, catch a flight back to Toronto?"

Alder unlocks the doors. "Why don't we start with a walk?"

Streetlights cast an orange glow across empty storefronts. Alder and I wander the sloping streets of downtown. The only places open are a couple of brew pubs. I munch on half a Clif bar and catch our reflection in one of the parked cars. "You know," I say to Alder. "I can't get into any of the bars around here."

"Me neither." Alder kicks a stray rock into the empty street. "Not for another couple months anyway. Last place I tried took my fake ID. That's what I get for being a local. Everyone already knows everyone."

A cool breeze runs past. I button up my cousin's flannel. "Then where are we going?"

"Why do we have to be *going* somewhere?" Alder shrugs his denim jacket. I flash a sideways glance and he laughs. "Okay, fine. I do have this spot we could check out. If you're not too drunk for an adventure."

"I think the ride sobered me up." I offer my hand and he takes it with ease. At his touch, warmth rushes into my cheeks.

We round the back of a closed-up corner store. The air is scented with rotting produce and latex garbage bags. Alder nods towards a low-hanging fire escape. "How good are you at climbing?"

I wrinkle my nose. "Not great."

"Good thing it's not too hard, then." He drops my hand and takes a running start onto the lid of a nearby dumpster. With a hop, he gives a hard yank and the metal ladder clatters down. Alder flashes me his half-moon smile. "Wanna go first?"

There's a twisting sickness in my stomach. Everything in my body is screaming to stay put. *This is a terrible idea*, I tell myself. *A terrible, rotten, poorly planned idea.*

I grip the bottom rung. The cold metal burns my palms. I go for the first step but my wet sneakers instantly slip. Alder braces me steady. He whispers, "You got this."

I try again. One step up, then another. The wind picks up and I squeeze my eyes shut. I don't know how long it takes. Finally, my hands find a flat, firm surface. In a scramble, I crawl forward onto the rooftop.

Alder appears at my side. "Nice work."

Fighting back the flurry in my stomach, I let him lead me to the ledge. Vernon spills out all around us. String-lights line the main street as the late-night crowd meanders home. Beyond downtown, a sprinkling of suburban homes turn off their porch lights one by one. It's like watching twinkling stars go out. Below, the lake rests silent; its smooth surface a mirror to the moon and the endless sky.

"It's beautiful," I whisper.

"Vernon always looks better from above." Alder moves a little closer. His fingers brush against mine. "Even more, when there's someone here to share the view."

That burning feeling reappears in the back of my

mouth. I wince. "Ugh. I'm never drinking again."

"I've heard that one before." Alder sets himself down. "Can't handle your liquor — just like Jer."

I prop myself up on one elbow. "How *do* you know my cousin, anyway?"

Alder shrugs. "We have a . . . history."

"What, you used to date or something?" I snort. Alder just stays quiet. My eyes go wide. "No! Really?!" I flip over like a fish out of water. "I didn't even know Jerry was . . . what, gay? Bi?"

Alder's gaze slips towards the sky. "I was a different person back then. You know how it is."

I hum in agreement, waiting for more. But Alder just changes the subject. He starts to point out the various sections of the city, the outlines of roads. He tells me about the geography of the mountains, local stories about the lake. It seems like he's got memories everywhere — the first place he got drunk, the time he tried to snowboard and ended up face-down in a bank.

I join in with my own anecdotes. I tell him about my home, my mothers and our little apartment in

Cabbagetown. It feels good to revisit those places, even just with my words. We puzzle our lives together until the horizon starts to hint periwinkle blue.

"It's nice to be able to talk to someone like this." Alder sets his hand on mine. "People around here act like they get it. But I've never actually been this close to someone . . . like me."

"Totally." I blush. "Same."

"Really?" Alder tilts his head. "I would've thought you met a lot, out in Toronto."

"Uh, right." I bite my tongue. Did I miss some kind of context? It seems too late to ask. "The thing is, I didn't really hang with anyone back home. Other than my moms, really. That's part of why I wanted to go somewhere new."

"I still can't believe you really did it." Alder gives a rough laugh. "Traded it all in."

I shrink my fingers back. "I guess I never thought about it like that."

"But that's what makes you so hardcore." Alder tucks towards me. "You just took off to do your own thing, not even a second thought to what it cost." He traces up my arm. "I'd be way too scared to try something like that. Especially in the last year of school — like, I'd have no clue how to do uni apps for next year without my folks around to help."

"Right. Next year." I pinch my eyes shut. That dizzy feeling is coming back. "Why didn't I think about next year?"

Alder's hands reach my cheek. "I've spent so long feeling like a ghost around here," he whispers. "Just wandering. Waiting. Trying to figure out how to start my life over." He studies my face. "And you just did the damn thing. You're incredible."

"I don't know if I would say that . . . " I answer but Alder's moving in. His lips push towards mine. I try to swallow my words down, focus on the moment. But the harder I try to pull close, the further I drift away.

I'm watching everything from a step outside, a second too late. All I can hear is the pounding of my heart, blood pumping in my ears. My held breath burns. It's like I'm drowning in the night air.

After a few seconds, Alder's eyes flutter open. "Are you okay?"

"Sorry — I'm fine." I choke on the lie. But I can't seem to figure out the truth either.

Alder furrows his brows. "You sure?"

"I'm fine," I say again, harder this time. "It's late. I should go."

Alder opens his mouth, then closes it again. "Of course," he says at last. "Let's get you home."

14 Residue

I THINK MY LATTE is decaf. Nestled against the foggy window of the Human Bean, I eye the barista and wonder if she misheard my order. Or maybe she got it wrong on purpose. Throat dry, I sip it anyway. I should've just got a tea.

Outside, pedestrians huddle under broad umbrellas beneath a grey sky. The space behind my eyes still aches like it did when I woke up. I've never had a hangover before. I never would've guessed it could be this bad.

The café's constant din is no help — clattering dishes, a constant barrage of small talk. Still, even all that can't drown the awful loop playing in my head.

I've run over every little detail of last night. Alder and I, silhouettes against the sky. His lips moving slow motion towards mine. *Rooftop . . . Moonlight . . . Hesitation.* I scribble the words into my notebook and wonder, "Why can't I just let you kiss me?"

"Well, you'd have to buy me brunch first!" Maggie appears over my shoulder. "Looks like *you* had a good night. Writing down all the best bits?"

I slap my notebook shut. "Not exactly."

Maggie shrugs and pulls out the seat across from mine. The chair's metal feet squeal and I wince. She holds it for Pippa, whose lips are pursed tight. "What happened last night?" she asks. "Your texts got all weird, then just stopped. We were worried."

"Well, one of us was. I figured you were just having fun." Maggie reaches over for a gulp of my latte. "Ugh, is that decaf?"

"Sorry." I rub sleep from my eyes. "I got distracted."

"I bet you did!" Maggie takes another swig. "Word is a *certain someone* gave you a ride home."

I blink up at her. "How did you —"

"Word spreads quick." Pippa side-eyes her girlfriend. "But we *weren't* going to bring it up."

"Don't stress." Maggie passes back my mug. "We've *all* been there."

"Have we?" Pippa raises her brows. "Look, Lucien, there's really no pressure to get into it . . ."

"Yes, pressure!" Maggie is teetering on the edge of her seat.

"Not much to say." I thumb the rim of my mug, tracing coffee stains. "Everything was going great . . . until it wasn't."

Pippa pushes closer. "Walk us through it, then," she tells me. "From the beginning."

I mean to tell them to drop it. I really do. But when I open my mouth, I start going on about my cousins, the party, the booze. Throwing up on Jerry's shoes. The warm seats in Alder's car. "He was saying all the right things," I tell them. "All romantic and stuff. But when we tried to kiss, I just . . . froze up."

"That's brutal, bud." Maggie picks at her teeth. "Was it like, he had really bad breath — or a booger hanging out?"

Pippa wrinkles her nose. "Did he say something super cliché and you just couldn't bring yourself to kiss that corny mouth?" Maggie shoots her a look. "What?"

"It wasn't like that." I lie my face against the table, cheek against cold plastic. "It was me. I'm just a broken, garbage person. Anytime I get close to someone, I ruin everything."

"Oh, shut up." Maggie shoves at my shoulder.

"Hey!" I whine. "I thought all my feelings were valid."

"Not that one." She makes a face at me. "Just because you don't wanna kiss someone doesn't have to be the end of the world. Maybe you're ace. Or demi, like Pippa."

"Or just not into that kind of thing," Pippa nods in agreement. "You don't have to put a label on it."

I peel myself up. "But it's not just when I'm kissing. Or, not-kissing." I tell them, "Anytime I get excited or nervous or just feel weird . . . My brain starts fizzing. My whole body like, freaks out."

The couple exchanges a quick glance. "That is a little more . . . challenging," Pippa admits. "But still doesn't mean that you ruined anything."

"You just had one awkward night," Maggie agrees. "Totally happens. Especially when someone you like is laying on the moves." Her gaze drifts towards the window. "You're on a rooftop and this major cutie is saying all this sweet stuff, about how you're so different . . ."

" . . . I don't remember mentioning the roof." My brows furrow. "Were you spying on my date again?!"

"No!" Pippa answers quickly. "Not this time, I promise. We just know the routine. Since Maggie and Alder had a thing for a bit. When she first moved here."

I sit there, waiting for the punchline of this poorly timed joke. Maggie just laughs, "I know. Weird, right?

He was more my type back then."

"Alder's even made a move on me once or twice." Pippa rolls her eyes, "But his lines work better when paired with that *moody-townie-shows-you-around routine.*"

"Routine?" The word is hollow in my mouth.

"More of a script?" Maggie pushes up her knee against the table. "He's just a relationship-hopper. Loves 'em and leaves 'em. Fun while it lasts, though."

"Yeah, real fun," says Pippa. My empty mug wobbles and she puts out a hand to stabilize it. "Until you catch him with a prep-school boy."

"Right. Well, that . . . " Maggie lets her chair fall back into place. "That was less fun."

My stomach lurches. It's like the world's going sideways again. "I feel sick."

"You need a bucket?" Maggie looks over her shoulder. "I think they have one in the bathroom."

"I can't believe I fell for it." I hold my gut, lip quivering. "He really made me think I was so special."

"You are!" says Pippa. "Just . . . in a general way."

"All those stories he told me." My nose pinches, anger rising in my throat. "The way he said he was so lonely. How scared he was to try and start over like I'm doing. I actually thought he was opening up!"

Maggie screws up her face. "That actually . . . doesn't sound so familiar." She leans over to Pippa. "Alder said he was *scared*?"

"Maybe he's learned some new moves." Pippa whispers back, "By the way, Mags, is this a bad time to say 'I told you so'?"

"Yes," I grumble.

"Um, speaking of bad timing." Maggie perks up. "Would this be the wrong spot to tell you, we got a gig?"

"Really?" I sniffle. "For your band?"

"Our duo." Pippa nods. "But we shouldn't even talk about it. We're not gonna take it."

"But it's basically a done deal!" Maggie drums her fingers. "We got a message this morning, from . . . what was the name? Sox?"

I grimace. "As in, Longbox Sox?"

Pippa's raised brows say it all. "They want us to open for *you-know-who*."

"He's not Voldemort," Maggie snorts. "But yeah, a certain *someone* passed around our Bandcamp. Now, they want us to play the next showcase!"

"We could say no." Pippa fiddles with her braid. "If it makes you uncomfortable."

"Yeah, right!" Maggie smacks her hands on the table. "Lucien's not gonna let personal drama get in the way of our musical careers!"

I swallow down the burning in my stomach. "I don't want to get in the middle of anything —"

"Then it's settled!" A smile pops across Maggie's cheeks. "Right, Pip?"

"Maybe." Pippa shrugs against her chair. "Even if we *could* get the songs together. And even if it wouldn't be *totally weird* opening for your ex. Are we actually ready to perform?"

"How long are you gonna worry about making things perfect?" Maggie pushes over to Pippa. "Things are almost never lined up exactly the way you'd want them.

Sometimes you just take what you get. Right, Lucien?"

"Maggie has a point," I admit. "Honestly, you should go for it."

"Really?" Pippa's mouth is a thin line. "You're sure?"

"Yeah." I nod. "Don't let my stuff with Alder get in the way of what you want to do."

"Hear that?" Maggie squeezes Pippa's shoulder. "We even got the boy's blessing!" Spinning back, she points towards me. "So can we rewind to the part where you yartzed all over Jerry's kicks? I'm gonna need that in perfect detail."

Pippa's frown softens. With a quiet laugh, she admits, "I did want to hear more about that."

My face cracks into a smile. "Well, okay." I start the story over. "There was this bottle I found in the basement . . ."

Around us, the café chatters on. Bells ring and orders come up. Customers flow through. Outside, drying raindrops catch hints of gold. The sun starts to make its way out again.

15 The Fall

FROZEN MOSS sticks to my jacket. I catch my breath against a pine tree. Alder waves from up ahead. I manage a weak smile in reply. The hiking trail's entrance is barely out of sight. I'm already worn through.

This isn't what I expected when Alder said he had a plan for our date. Then again, I guess I don't know what to expect from him. When he glances back again, wisps of his silver hair sparkle in the sunlight. My heart starts to race. "Don't fall for him," I remind myself in a whisper. "This is all just fun."

"What's that?" Alder calls out.

"I said," I push myself up, "this is so fun!"

"I know, right?!" Alder laughs and plows ahead. I follow his boot prints with my sneakers. Maggie's advice plays over in my head. *Take what you get.* So what if Alder isn't perfect? Sure, his moves might be practiced and cheesy. But we can still enjoy our time together, while it lasts. It's not like I plan on staying in Vernon forever.

"Isn't that awesome?" Alder pauses to admire a huge cedar that leans at an impossible angle. Roots tangled around a massive stone, its bark broken open with tiny mushrooms peeking through. "So cool!"

All I can think of is how that *so-cool* tree looks like it could fall and crush us at any moment. "Let's keep moving," I say.

"Totally!" Alder skips ahead. "I bet they don't have trails like this out east."

I speak into the neck of my jacket, "Sure don't."

In truth, it is kind of a nice walk. Alder rattles off

tips about the forest — how to spot the trails of little creatures, the best ways to climb over tricky rocks. In the warmer spots, sun shines through the trees to reveal a series of thin streams. Patches of ice give way with satisfying snaps.

At last, we brush aside a few low-hanging branches and arrive at a small clearing. Along one edge, a half-frozen waterfall is decorated with long icicles. On the other side, a view of the valley. Budding pastures, the sharp outlines of highways. Vernon sits quiet, a web of suburban homes. The silent traffic of the city centre glitters in the midday sun.

"Wow . . ." I whisper. "You can see everything from up here."

"Yeah." Alder's eyes stay on me. "It's quite the view."

"Yeah, right." I roll my eyes and prop myself up on a rock. For a while, I just listen to the sound of the waterfall. "Seriously. This is a great spot. Thanks for showing me."

Alder shrugs. "I used to come here a lot. Whenever I had really heavy stuff on my mind."

IN A HEARTBEAT

"Right, sure." I fight back a laugh. "What do you even have to stress about?" When Alder turns, I expect to catch that classic grin of his. Instead, there's hurt in his eyes. "Sorry," I mutter. "I didn't mean to say you don't have problems . . ."

"It's cool." Alder kicks at the frosted ground. "I guess I don't really show it. When your folks are a couple of shrinks, you learn to put up a good front."

"What do you mean?" I scooch aside, making room for Alder to sit beside me. "I figured they'd be understanding about . . . stressy stuff, or whatever."

"That's the problem." Alder picks at a corner of the rock. "They're *too* understanding." A few pebbles come off in his hand. Alder flicks them towards the city below, one by one. "I made the mistake of telling them I was depressed when I was like, thirteen. Ever since, they're always monitoring me — every slip-up with my grades, any weekend I sleep in. I must've tried a dozen therapies and techniques." He tosses aside the remaining stones with a rough laugh. "You can only imagine how they reacted when I came out."

I grimace. "Was it bad?"

"Worse. They were *worried*." Alder's eyes stay fixed on the horizon. "They knew all the stats. Bullying, self-harm, suicide . . . That's when they switched me to home school."

"Do you like it?" I ask. "Homeschooling?"

Alder chews over my question. "I like being able to take my time with things," he decides. "Gets lonely, though."

"What about your band?" I point out. "You get to hang out with them, play whenever."

Alder shrugs. "With guys like that, it's not really the same . . ." His voice trails as he turns to meet my eyes. "Not like with you."

"Come on." I smirk but Alder's face stays still. He just studies me, then gently reaches over to touch my hand.

"Don't you feel it too?" he asks. And despite everything, I do.

My heart is pounding. A breeze rustles through the treetops. They sing like falling rain. A thought drifts across my mind: *I wonder how many people have fallen for that line.*

Maggie and Pippa's words of warning bounce around in my head. I should be careful, not get too serious. It's all just a game. Just fun. I can have fun, right?

I push a hand against his chest and give what I hope is an alluring smile. "I sure feel *something* when I'm with you."

"What —" Alder starts to ask but I don't wait a second longer. Eyes squeezed shut, I smash my face forward. Our mouths crash against each other, the clack of butting teeth. There's a sudden rush of warmth and a copper taste. Alder cries out, "Ow!"

I yank myself back. His hand is at his lip. "Oh, crap! Did I just —? I'm so sorry!"

"It's okay," Alder mumbles. "I'm fine."

"That was so stupid." I tremble to my feet. "I'm so stupid. I should go."

He gives a weak laugh. "I drove us here, remember?"

"I can call for a ride." I start walking backwards.

"Really, it's the least I can —" The back of my sneaker catches the water's edge and a second later, I smack backwards, right into the waterfall.

A cascade of icicles splash around me. My sneakers and jeans get soaked through. Alder's strong arms pull me back and check me over. I sputter, shiver, struggle to catch my breath. "You're okay," he tells me. "Just got the wind knocked out of you. Breathe out, then in. That's it. Again."

We lie there, breathing and holding each other. In the warmth of his chest, I can hear his heartbeat. Mine slows to match it in time.

He gives a tender kiss to my forehead. "How are you feeling now?"

"Cold," I answer, throat raw.

"No kidding," he laughs. "Let's go get you out of those wet clothes."

16 Bruised Not Broken

DOUBLE SHOWERHEADS sear hot water against my back. Arms wrapped tight, I force myself not to move. This is my punishment for initiating possibly the worst first kiss of all time. Surrounded by steam, I sit and watch water circle the drain. When my toes and fingers start to prune, I step out. By the door, a towel and fresh clothes sit inside a plastic bag.

With shaking hands, I dry off and squeeze into my binder. Thankfully, it's only somewhat damp. Once my chest is properly snug, I shrug into a warm pair of sweatpants and a hoodie. The clothes smell like Alder and my heart can't help but flutter.

The rest of my wet clothes get shovelled into the crinkling plastic. From my jeans pocket, my notebook falls to the tile floor. It's waterlogged. My stomach sinks as I flip through ink-smeared pages. So much for finding inspiration on this trip. I'll be lucky if I can recover even half of these fragmented poems.

In Alder's socks, I tiptoe into the hallway. I find a living room with no one living in it. White upholstery couches, a clear coffee table with a bowl of untouched fruit. Books on child psychology rest across the mantle of an electric fireplace. Everything in this house looks like it cost a month of my mothers' rent, or more.

In the kitchen, I peek through cupboards and drawers. Sparkling plates, matching sets of cutlery, what looks like an unused immersion blender. In a drawer of elastic bands and scissors, there's a handful of photos loose from their frames. They show a young, girlish person with jet-black hair. Alder never mentioned having a sister. She looks just like him, except there's no sign of that wry smile he wears so well.

"Honey?" I spin around and find a tall woman, a tea kettle in hand. I recognize her from the photos. Must be Alder's mother. She lifts a mug towards me. " . . . Do you take honey in your tea?"

"No!" I shut the drawer behind my back. "Um. Well, yes. But I don't need any —"

"Son, is that you?!" A short man with a thick moustache pops through the back door. "I need your hand in the garage . . . Oh!" He stops short, "You're not Alder, are you?" I shake my head and he just laughs. "Well, never a bad time for tea and company. Camilla, good to see you've already got the kettle going!"

"I was just saying I don't need any tea . . ."

"Nonsense!" Alder's father has those same golden eyes. His face is pinched with wrinkles when he smiles. "I've already heard all about your dip in the waterfall. You need a hot bevvy after something like that, I should know! Why, when I took on the Baikal marathon —"

"Reg, please." Camilla's smile is just like Alder's. "Do you *have* to tell that story every time we have a guest?"

"It's *relevant* this time!" Alder's dad insists.

"Really, it's okay." I step back. "I've messed up enough of your day."

Camilla purses her lips. "Do you always engage in such negative self-talk?"

"*Mom.*" Alder appears in the doorway with a groan. "Can you turn it off for, like, a second?" He holds an ice pack to his fat lip.

"Sorry, kiddo," Reg chuckles.

"Why don't we all share in some collective breathing exercises?" says Camilla. "I'll start." She lifts her hands to her chest and takes a deep breath in. Reg joins in with a long exhale. Alder grabs my arm and pulls me away.

"They seem nice," I whisper.

"Yeah," Alder grumbles. "It's exhausting."

Alder's bedroom is bathed in sunlight. Across his desk, a spattering of textbooks and loose paper. In the corner sits a cherry-red guitar and two others on a three-prong rack. The walls are covered in posters: Janelle Monáe, the Weeknd. There's even one signed by Laura Jane Grace! Alder hops over piles of laundry and falls onto the bed. "If I had known you were coming," he says, "I would've cleaned up. Or at least shoved some stuff under my bed."

Alder motions for me to join him. Gingerly, I sit down on the corner of his queen-size mattress, still holding tight to the plastic bag of my wet clothes. Alder flips through a stack of records on his side-table. I start to suggest, "Maybe I should go call for a ride?"

"One sec." Alder turns on a small, orange record player. He sits up. "Close your eyes for this. Trust me."

A song begins to swell between us. I let my eyes fall shut. Notes are plucked like raindrops. Distant drums, growing stronger. "Try breathing out with the beat," says Alder. I follow his instructions and a shiver runs down my spine. The music runs through me, spiralling around us. Finally, the song ends and I blink as if waking up from a dream. Alder asks, "Feel better?"

"Actually, yeah," I tell him. "I do."

Alder gives his sideways smile. "That's one of my favourites for when I'm stressed out. Really gets you grounded, you know?" Behind him, the record hums on its spinning track. "What about you?"

"What about me?" I chuckle.

Alder asks, "What do you do to chill yourself out?"

"I don't usually *do* anything," I answer with a shrug. "I guess that's kinda the problem. I just sort of . . . freeze up. Or I try to power through, which usually makes everything even worse."

"Been there." Alder offers his hands. "Can I show you something from my annoying therapy stuff that actually kinda works?" I nod, letting him rest his palms in mine. "Start with a breath out. Good. Now, what are five things you can see?"

I give an awkward laugh. "Um, you?"

Alder raises his brows. "Now, four more."

Glancing around, I shrug out a few more answers. "The ceiling? Floor. Wall . . . Records."

"Nice," says Alder. "Now, four things you can touch."

I flex my fingers. "Can your hands count as two?"

Alder laughs, gentle and sweet. "Sure."

"And . . ." I shimmy my hips. "Bed. Duvet."

"Three things you can hear?" he asks. The record's on a new song now, one with a quicker pace.

"Guitar. Drums." I give a long exhale. "My heart. I can hear that too."

Alder slips one hand up my arm. "Two things you can smell?"

"How am I supposed to —"

"Just try," he whispers.

I inhale deeply. "I can smell . . . your breath. And mine."

"Final question." Alder cups my cheek. "What's one thing you can taste?"

I meet his lips with mine. He winces and I pull back. "Oh, crap. I'm sorry, was I not supposed to — ?"

"It's fine," Alder chuckles, nursing his swollen lip. "Better than fine."

Slowly, I kiss him again. This time, on his cheek. I trace his face, down his neck. My hands slide towards his waist. We lie back against the mountain of pillows on his bed. His breath is pressed into my neck. I feel him moan against me.

When the record finally reaches its end, I whisper, "Wow. I've never done anything like that before."

Alder grins. "I'm honoured."

"And that count-down thing." I prop myself up. "That's really cool. I wonder if I could make a poem that way . . . "

"I'd love to read your words," says Alder. "If you'd ever like to share."

"I actually have my notebook with me!" As soon as I mention it, I want to swallow the words back up. "Uh, not that you have to read it right now, or anything . . ."

"Are you kidding?" Alder sits up. "Of course I do!"

My stomach is tight as I shuffle through the wet

mess that was my date outfit. Once I find my notebook, Alder stays quiet as he flips through the soggy pages of my sorry poetry. "I know, it's a mess," I tell him. "Literally." After another few minutes of silence, I stammer, "You know what, never mind. This was a bad idea."

"This . . . it's . . ." His golden eyes sparkle. "It's amazing."

I roll my eyes. "You don't have to tease me."

"I'm not! The metaphors, your overlapping imagery . . . " Glancing up, a smile crosses Alder's face. "Have you ever thought of putting this to music?"

17 Lovestained

THE SIDEWALKS OF VERNON are slick after a long rain. Sprigs of fresh grass sprout between the cracks. The air is hazy and thick, the sun a narrow dot in the midday sky. I skip down the hill towards the city centre.

A gust of wind shuffles past. I pull my hands into the sleeves of Alder's hoodie. Alder let me wear it home the day of my waterfall fiasco. Hard to believe that was two weeks ago. I've hardly taken off the hoodie since. Breathing in deep, I can still smell him in the fabric. A rush of warmth runs up my neck. In the pocket of the sweater, I feel the gentle weight of my journal. I give it a soft pat of reassurance. Today's the day my scattered thoughts become a song.

We've been meaning to meet up for a while now. There's been little progress on our songwriting since Alder hatched the idea. Back and forth, we suggested places and times but none ever seemed to fit. Cafés are too crowded. His parents' house, too quiet. Alder's certain Reg and Camilla would listen in the whole time. The McMartin residence was out of the question for too many reasons to name.

Not to mention, anytime we do manage to get together . . . Well, songwriting hasn't been at the top of the to-do list. We usually get caught up talking, telling stories or just making out. I blush just at the memory of his lips on mine. We haven't gone any further than kissing, but I never knew kissing could go so far.

Today we're finally making it happen. Alder managed to book some rehearsal time at Longbox

Records. The show is just a couple days away and Alder wants the song to be his opening number. A big debut, for us both. My heart should be racing with panic. Instead, I catch my reflection in the window of the Human Bean and find I'm smiling.

I wave to the barista on the other side of the glass. She gives back a flat nod in reply. There's a skip in my step as I move down the main street. Something tells me this is going to be a great day.

Frankie is in his usual spot, chowing down on a Tim Hortons sandwich. I stop for a quick hello and pass over a handful of change. "Thank you, young lady," he tells me. "Stay dry, now. Storm's coming in later."

"You take care, sir!" I wave.

At last, I duck into the alley that leads to Longbox. As I push through the glass entrance, its broken bell gives a muted announcement of my arrival. The place still smells of dusty jackets and unvacuumed carpet. I breathe in deep and head into the maze of milk crates and uneven stacks. Sox's counter comes into view but the clerk is nowhere to be seen. Neither is Alder. I must be early.

IN A HEARTBEAT

The backroom door is open. A pair of voices drifts around its edge. "I'm telling you," says one. "It was maybe the worst yet. A total crapshoot."

"Hardly seems worth it, after a certain point," says another in a whisper. "I can't believe you kept at it." The two laugh, casual and friendly.

With careful steps, I move in closer and peek through the doorway on its hinge side. My heart kicks up a beat. It's Alder, perched on a stack of crates, guitar in hand. "Honestly, me neither," he says. "It gets super cringey sometimes. Like you wouldn't believe."

Is he talking about me? I wonder. I know our first few dates were sort of awkward. *No,* I tell myself. *He's just complaining about something else.* I'm sure of it.

There's a sigh from beyond where I can see. "You know this isn't helping, right?"

"Sorry." Eyes on the fretboard, Alder plucks out a gentle tune. "But, honestly, if I had to do it all again, I'm not sure I'd be up for it. It's not even just the trans stuff, though that doesn't help either."

My stomach drops. *Did someone out me to him?*

"Maybe you're right." The other person stands and my eyes go wide. What's Pippa doing here? "This whole thing was probably a mistake," she says. "At least it's not too late to call it off. I should talk to Maggie first though . . ."

"No — wait." Alder looks up quickly. He sets down the guitar and runs a hand through his bangs. "Listen, I'm not doing a good job of this."

Pippa gives a sigh. "It's all so overwhelming." She pulls at her braid. "I don't know if I have it in me."

"Let me show you something." Alder offers his hands. "It'll help calm your nerves." I feel my cheeks begin to burn as Pippa follows his instructions. "First, take a breath. Now, look around for five things you can see . . ."

My fingernails dig into my arm. I feel a bubbling in the back of my throat, rising to my lips.

"Can I help you?" There's a voice from behind. I jump and turn to find Sox, arms full of unwashed coffee cups.

"Sorry!" My voice squeaks and I stumble back. I smack against the backroom door and slam it shut.

A second later, there's a knock. The door handle jiggles slightly, followed by a push.

I freeze in place. Heart pounding in my chest. Sox watches with half-lidded interest as they start to stow away the mugs.

"Hello?" Pippa's muffled voice calls out, "Is someone there?"

All at once, my body kicks into high gear. I take off, leaping over Sox and around the counter. The momentum takes me sideways into one of the shelves. Several records skitter across the floor. I don't have time to pick them up.

Behind me, Alder's voice. "Lucien? Is that you?"

I'm already out the door. Humid air hits my face. I slump against the alley's brick wall but only for a second. If I wait any longer, there could be footsteps. Questions. Heart pounding in my chest, I take off up the hill as fast as my legs will carry me. Through clenched teeth, I curse myself. For knowing better. But falling for him anyway. *How could I have been so stupid?*

"It's alive!" Elbow over the back of the couch, George raises a soda to toast my emergence from the basement.

18 Numb

I SHUFFLE PAST in slippers, blanket draped around my shoulders.

"Have a good sleep, little dude?" Jerry's feet sit against the coffee table as he flips through the TV channels. "You almost beat Joey's record for sleeping in."

"Don't call me little," I grumble under my breath.

"Stop changing so fast!" Joey barks at his brother, wrestling for the remote.

I head for the kitchen. From behind, I catch a hint of Jean's voice. "Be nice, boys. I don't think Lucien's feeling well."

On my toes to reach the top cabinet, I pull down a box of crackers, a jar of peanut butter and some chocolate chips. When I stumble back through the main room, Jean makes room for me on the couch. "Come, sit down, Lucien," she offers. "We could watch a . . . documentary?"

I pull the blanket over my head. "I'm gonna go lie down."

Stepping down the basement stairs, I push the door shut behind me. It slams harder than I planned. I hang there for a second, waiting to see if I'm about to get told off. Or maybe asked if I'm okay. There's only the quiet creak of the stairs beneath my feet, the muffled sounds of an argument. No one is coming.

The basement's solitary window paints pale grey light across my makeshift bedroom. I land face first on the futon. Heavy footfalls wander across the ceiling. I tear into the box of crackers — the label exclaims that they're *cheddar-blasted*. I smear peanut butter on top and add a handful of chocolate chips. It tastes terrible. I go in for seconds.

My phone screen lights up with a series of incoming messages. I don't bother to read them before swiping them aside. There's nothing to be said.

"I guess they were right," I admit to the empty room. "Alder's a player, just using the same old moves to get what he wants. Until he moves along to the next new thing." Scowling into the peanut butter jar, I push back tears. "And I'm the fool who fell for him. Even though I knew better."

It's still hard to believe. That Alder has known the whole time, about me, about everything. I knew our dates were awkward but I never thought he'd be laughing about them behind my back. With Pippa, of all people! I think about calling Maggie, warning her that Alder's trying to make a move. But no. "They've got to be in on it together," I tell myself. "It's the only thing that makes sense."

Setting up that awful first date, pressuring me to

go to the party. "All so they can laugh at the new kid." My teeth dig into my lip, almost breaking skin. "It's all been lies on lies."

I chew on that last line — *lies on lies*. Maybe I can at least get some poetry out of this whole miserable affair. Tossing aside my stolen snacks, I reach for Alder's hoodie. A faint smell of him still hangs around the collar. I try to swallow down the heartache, rooting through the pocket for my notebook.

It's not there. I try my backpack, the pockets of my favourite jeans. Nothing. My casual search turns into full-on panic. I tear through every possible place it could be, and a few impossible ones too. It's gone.

"Perfect." I fall into the blankets and roll up tight. "Just perfect."

My phone lights up again with a call. Who calls people these days? I go to swipe it away but stop short when I see the name paired with the incoming FaceTime.

"My baby!" Mom screeches with excitement and the video shakes. I catch a glimpse of Ma trying to gain control.

I wipe cheddar-blasted crumbs from my cheeks. "I didn't think we had a call planned for today."

"We didn't," says Ma. Her thumb covers half the lens. "We just missed you so much, your mother said we should be spontaneous." Ma sets down the phone. "True fashion for an Aries-rising."

Mom gives a flip of her crimson hair. "But it was my Pisces-moon that told me you would answer!"

Ma peers over my shoulder. "Have you been drinking enough water?" I lift up my Nalgene, half empty. "Good." She nods in approval. "Now, tell us everything."

"Everything!" Mom repeats. "Are your auntie and uncle treating you okay? Have you made any new friends over there?"

"It's great," I say through my teeth. There's a loud thud from up above, followed by raised voices. "Really, really . . . great."

"And school, your studies?" Mom shouts as she disappears off camera. Off screen, I hear a blender pulse.

"Well, it's definitely different from back home." I eye the stack of unfinished assignments sitting in the corner of my room. "I've got a handle on it, though. Definitely."

"What about your room?" Ma leans so close to the camera, I can see right up her nose again. "You haven't shown us any pictures. Do you have a nice view?"

A draft sneaks along the edge of my basement window. "Actually, about that . . ."

"It sounds like you're adjusting really well!" Mom reappears, smoothie in hand. She sips on a metal straw. "Wish we could say the same for Jeanette."

"Mel." Ma flashes a stern look. "We said we wouldn't bring it up."

I had almost forgotten. Jean's daughter is living in my room. Even if I wanted to move back home, I wouldn't have a place to stay. "Is she having a hard time starting at U of T?"

"The first few years in a new place are always hard," says Ma. She nabs the smoothie and takes a sip.

A pit opens up in my stomach. "The first few *years*?"

Mom tries to pull her drink back, but only manages to spill a few chunks of fruit onto the camera lens. She wipes off the phone with her shirt. "Of course, you're the exception to the rule." She smiles into the camera. "Clearly, you're thriving out there."

"No, I'm not." My voice breaks into a blubbery sob. "I'm doing terrible!" The words fall out of me all at once. "The food is awful and the people are mean. And everything is wet and weird and small and I hate it here! I just want to go home!"

There's a light knock on the wall. Jean stands there, dinner plate in hand. She stares at me for a few seconds, then crosses the room in silence and sets down the food before disappearing again.

"Shit," I whisper and start to get up. "Wait, Aunt Jean, I didn't mean it like that." I can hear her heading back up the stairs. "I'm sorry," I tell my mothers. "I think I should go."

"Don't you dare!" Mom snaps through the phone. "My sister's always been the type to take things too personally. Let her sulk."

Ma jumps in. "What I think your mom is *trying* to say is . . ." She lifts the phone, wrinkles of concern across her forehead. ". . . Is that your aunt Jean is a grown woman. She can take care of herself. Right now, we need to focus on you. Why didn't you tell us sooner that things aren't okay?"

"I don't know." I shuffle my feet against the cold floor. "I didn't want to let you down."

"Lucien," Ma says my name without hesitation. "You're our child. We're always going to be proud of you."

In the background of the phone screen, Mom is puttering around. "Now, your Ma and I will need some time to get things ready." She flips open her laptop and starts scrolling through flight listings. "Think you can wait one more week before we bring you home?"

My voice wavers. "You'd really do that?"

Mom looks up briefly. "Well, we're not just going to leave you out there to suffer!"

"Now," Ma sits back down and pulls the phone closer. "Tell us everything. Seriously, this time."

19 Quiet Motions

THE ERASER END of my pencil taps on my desk, math quiz still half empty. My thoughts hum back and forth like angry bees caught in a glass jar. If I ever knew the answers to these questions, I can't remember them now.

I rub sleep from my eyes. I meant to study last night, I really did. Somehow the whole evening just got away from me. I had a stomach-ache after dinner, as usual, so I spaced out on my phone for a few hours. Next thing I knew, I'd fallen asleep. In my dreams, I was running on a moving road, legs far too slow. A huge cloud was chasing after me. I woke up tired.

Along the margin of my math test, I write, *Spent all night chasing clouds.* More words slip edgewise from my pencil, like a tree losing its leaves. *Falling through . . .*

"Pencils down!" orders a voice from the front.

No, that's not right. I cross out the second line and try again. *Scattered. Uprooted. Swept away.*

"Lucien?" Ms. Schmitke says my name like it's an accusation. Lips tight, she glances at the pencil in my grip.

"Sorry," I mumble back. The bell rings for next period. On my way out, my unfinished quiz gets stacked along with the rest on Ms. Schmitke's desk. So go the bits of my almost-poem. I don't know why I bothered to write them down anyway. Without my notebook, there doesn't seem to be much point.

Eyes down, I count my steps. The chattering sounds of the high school hallway are muffled. It's like I'm on the inside of a fishbowl and someone's tapping on the glass.

"Buddy!" A hand takes my arm. "Didn't you hear

me calling you?" asks Maggie, hand on hip. "Mountain air messing with your ears?"

"Hey." I shrug my backpack over one shoulder. "Just heading home for lunch."

"Again?" Pippa arrives at my side. She's got new, cat-eye glasses. They bring out the sharp lines of her face. "If you don't have bagged lunch, I can share mine."

"It's cool." I move towards the exit. "Thanks, anyway."

The couple paces after me. "You're still coming to the show tonight," says Pippa. "Right?"

"Of course, he's coming!" Maggie walks backwards with ease. "Tonight, Longbox Records. Tomorrow, world tour!"

I answer with a shrug. "You know how Jean is about family dinner. I'll have to ask her."

"Dude, seriously?" Maggie steps in my way. "This is our first real gig. Plus, *you-know-who*'s gonna be there." She wiggles her eyebrows at me. "Don't you wanna see your boy-toy?"

"Whatever." Shoulder first, I push towards the

exit. I can feel both of them watching as I go.

Rainwater runs in thin streams along the sloping sidewalk. A puddle edges into my sneakers. It's only been a couple months since I arrived in Vernon, but every part of me is worn through. Maybe Ma will buy me new shoes when I get home.

The McMartin house is mercifully quiet. I grab an egg-salad sandwich from the kitchen and toss my bag aside. From the half-closed zipper of my backpack, a folded scrap of paper tumbles out. I pick it up and find a doodle of Ms. Schmitke inside, her face a red balloon that's hissing out equations. I chuckle. Maggie must have slipped it in before I left.

A pang of guilt hits me in the chest. I still haven't told her I'm leaving. There's no way to know if she was in on everything with Pippa and Alder, or if she's getting played too. At this point, I'm not sure there's much I can do either way.

My phone hums on the dining-room table. Probably Maggie, ripping my head off for snapping at them. It vibrates again. Maybe Pippa, pre-apologizing for Maggie. The third time, I reach for it. It must be Ma with an update on travel plans. She said flights were pricey but they'd figure it out. At this point, I'd take three layovers over another night in that frigid basement.

A whispered voice speaks through the phone. "Look outside." A knock on the window makes me jump. Alder is there, a weak smile and a wave.

I stand frozen, eyes wide. "How did you even —"

"A little birdy told me you've been having lunch at home." He holds up a tote bag. "I brought you something. Can I come in?"

Before I can answer, he's already around and through the door. "Just like I remember it," he chuckles. "Figures, Jean doesn't seem the type for changing things up too much. Hey, are they still 'renovating' the basement?"

I take a step back. "What're you doing here?"

"Right, sorry." Alder fumbles with the canvas tote and passes it to me. "I was just cleaning out some stuff at home. Thought you might want some of it."

"What, now I'm your charity case?" I huff and

keep my arms crossed. "Or is this a trash dump?"

"More like an apology?" Alder unpacks the bag himself. He sets a pair of gloves on the table along with a box of chamomile tea.

I eye him carefully. "For . . . ?"

"Everything?" Alder pulls off his toque. His silver bangs have grown jet-black roots. "For pressuring you into anything or making you feel weird . . . I just really like you. But I totally get if you just want to be friends." His golden eyes search mine. "Do you . . . want to be friends?"

I roll my eyes, my hip leaning against the table. "You can drop the act."

A passing pain slips across Alder's face. "I'm serious." He inches closer. "You're one of the coolest people I've ever met. Like, totally brave and —" To that, I let out a harsh laugh. But Alder keeps going. "I mean it! Everyone always talks about running away, starting over. But you actually did it."

"I said, stop it with the lines!" I snap at him. "I'm not falling for this again. I heard you talking to Pippa the other day." My nose pinches, but I swallow back the pressure. "I know you've just been messing with me, or whatever."

Brows furrowed, Alder searches my face. "With Pippa?"

His fake ignorance only feeds the fire inside me. "I heard everything! How you've been suffering through our 'cringey' dates and 'the whole trans thing.'" With a hard twist, I start to stomp away from him. "I don't know why you picked me for your stupid prank. But, hey, you win. I'm leaving."

"Lucien." Alder's voice breaks when he calls my name. "For once, just stay."

Cheeks burning, I scowl back at him.

"Listen," he tells me, "I wasn't talking to Pippa about you. I was talking about *me*."

20 Things Still Left to Say

"I'LL ADMIT, sometimes I fall into a script with people, I guess," says Alder. I've never seen him so shrunken as he looks sitting in the dining chair next to mine. "I don't know. It's easier that way." He screws up his mouth, testing out each word as it comes. "Like a song, you can practise. I won't screw up if I rehearse it enough. If I know all the parts."

Gripping my elbows, I lean back in my seat. "Can you see why that's kinda messed up?"

"I really am sorry, Lucien." Alder's face falls. "When I'm with you, it's like I get thrown off my rhythm. In a good way." There's a faint laugh in his voice. "You've got like, zero tolerance for bullshit."

My eyes study every inch of his expression, looking for hints of a lie. In the silence between us, Alder drums his fingers along the table. "So," he says eventually, "you really didn't know . . . about me?"

I toss up my hands. "How would I have known?"

"I just figured." Alder shrugs. "The way word travels around here. Plus, I was being pretty obvious." He raises a tentative brow. "You are too, though, right?"

"No!" I snap and pinch my eyes shut. "I mean, no, it was not obvious. Yes, I am too." With a sigh, I slump back. "Is this whole freaking city trans?"

A laugh breaks Alder's sombre expression. "Maybe we just have a way of finding each other." He reaches for the tote sprawled across the table. "Speaking of . . . I brought you something else." From the bag, he pulls a tight, cropped top. "I hope it's not too forward . . ."

"Is that a binder?" I take the compression vest from his hands. The design is beautiful, a series of glittering flowers and budding leaves. "You don't need it?"

"I figured you could use a spare. And I have way too many." Alder shakes his head. "Dad got the idea to sign up for a Shapeshifters subscription box. I get a new binder, like, once a month."

I hold up the binder. It looks like the right size. "That honestly sounds awesome."

"Just let me know if you ever need, like, twenty trans flags." Alder leans back, a hand on his own chest. "Plus, I won't need the binders for much longer. My folks decided they're gonna pay for my top surgery when I turn nineteen."

My eyes go wide. "That's amazing!"

"I know, right?" Alder runs a hand through his bangs. "They've been reading up on it for months. Finally picked a private clinic out in Toronto." He peeks up at me. "Maybe you can show me around when I'm out there?"

There's a sinking feeling in my stomach. I'd almost

forgot, I'm supposed to be leaving soon. I run my hands across the binder's fabric. "So that stuff you were saying to Pippa. It was really just advice?"

"Despite how it may seem," Alder says with a shrug, "there's not actually that many trans artists around these parts. I just wanted to give her a heads-up on the scene."

"Well. Good." I bite my lip. "Because I was . . . pretty jealous, honestly. I like you a lot. Though, I know we never actually talked about being exclusive."

"But we should." Alder offers his hand. "Whether we keep it open or try the monogamy thing, I want you to know, there's no one else like you in my life."

My heart rushes. But before either of us can say more, there's the drone of a car pulling into the driveway. "I think someone's home," I whisper. "You should go."

Alder stands and roots through his jacket pocket. "Just one more thing." He pulls out a small, stained notebook. "I think you dropped this at Longbox."

My mouth falls open. "You had it this whole time?"

"I wanted to return it!" Alder laughs. "But *someone* wasn't taking my calls." He passes it to me. "I hope you don't mind, I started composing that song —"

Keys jingle in the doorway. I can hear Jean humming to herself.

"Crap," I whisper. "Go! Hide!"

Alder dives into the kitchen just as Jean swings open the door. I pull out my phone, pretending to scroll. "Oh, hey, Auntie," I say in what I hope is a casual tone. "What're you doing home?"

"I heard you were walking home for lunch hour." Jean slips off her heels. "Thought I'd come fix you something and we could have a little chat." She steps towards the kitchen.

"No!" I bolt up. "I, uh, already got something."

Jean frowns at me, just long enough for Alder to sneak into the hall. "Well, it's my lunch hour too." She clicks her tongue and heads to the fridge.

"Right," I mumble. "Of course." Alder sneaks into the front hall.

"So I have some good news." Jean's face pops

into the kitchen window. "Jerry's moving in with his girlfriend!"

"Jerry has a girlfriend?" I snort. "I mean, that's great."

"That means Jeanette's room will be free!" Jean pulls out a container of leftovers. "For your next visit, that is."

"Great," I say, half listening. From the corner of my eye, I catch Alder ducking behind the coat rack.

"I know things haven't been all that easy for you." Jean comes to sit beside me, sliding a plate of leftover lasagna in front of her. "But we've really enjoyed having you here." Breath tight, I nod as Alder moves silently towards the door. "You know, you really are just like your mother. Always hurrying off to the next adventure."

"Mhm?" I bite at the inside of my cheeks. Alder is reaching for the door handle.

"I used to resent her for it." Jean pokes at her meal. "Rushing off to see the world while I stayed behind to take care of Mom and Dad." She lets out a long sigh. "But that's all behind us now." She pats my hand. "And I want you to know, we'll always have a seat for you at our table."

"Thank you." I squeeze Jean's hand.

There's a faint click as Alder sneaks the door open. A second later, he scampers past the window. "Well, would you look at that!" Jean turns and I freeze in place. She nods towards the clock. "We used up our whole lunch hour just gabbing! Do you need a ride back?"

Relief washes over me. "That would be great," I tell her as we stand to leave. "Oh, and I've been meaning to ask you, there's this show later tonight . . ."

21 Come What May

IN THE COLD of the alleyway, waves of steam and music drift out into the early night. I hover at the entrance to Longbox Records. My gloved hand lingers against the glass. A poster taped to the foggy window reads: *Longbox Showcase. One night only.*

Even in the warmth of an early spring night, my fingers are chilled. A weight sinks in my stomach as I linger at the record shop entrance. Maybe it was a mistake to come. After the way I've been with Maggie and Pippa, do they even want to see me? And then there's Alder . . .

"You made it," says a familiar voice in my ear. I turn and Alder's golden eyes send shivers up my spine.

"Shouldn't you be inside already?" I ask.

"Sox can hold them off for a minute." He shrugs. "Besides, we're still waiting on some talent."

"We're here!" hollers Pippa, tripping over herself as she stumbles towards us. Her arms hold a massive binder, paper spilling out its sides. "We made it," she gasps. "I got everything."

"Well, most of everything." Maggie appears a second later. She lugs a long, rectangular bag under one arm. "We got halfway here before *someone* realized she forgot our music."

"You were supposed to put it in the piano bag!" Pippa hisses at her partner, then catches herself. Jaw clenched, she takes a deep breath and lets it out slowly. "It doesn't matter," she says. "We're probably too late anyway."

"As if," Alder chuckles. "Come on, I'll help you get set up."

As Pippa passes by, she nods to me with a nervous smile. "It's good to see you," she whispers.

"Yeah," Maggie agrees. She shoves her shoulder into mine. "I knew you wouldn't ditch us!"

"You kidding?" I push open the door for the four of us. "I wouldn't miss this for the world."

The air of Longbox is thick with noise and people. Shoulder-to-shoulder, punks and hipsters sort through shelves of records and sip drinks from mason jars. My heart races as I step into the crowd, heartbeat pounding in my head. A cold feeling sneaks into my knees, locking my legs tight. But then, I feel Alder's hand in mine. He gives me a squeeze and we take a deep breath. On the exhale, we move forward, together.

"You've got your phone?" Jean's hands grip the steering wheel. We weave through the streets of Vernon. Daylight glints off the windshield and dances through budding trees. I let my window sit open, soaking in the sunshine.

"Yep." I pat the pocket of my jeans.

"And your bag?" She looks over her shoulder briefly before we turn off from the main street. The car chugs slightly as the road grows steep, curving up. "Where is it?"

"In the back," I tell her. "Just like it was five minutes ago."

"Right. Good." She gives a curt nod. We pull past mountain homes, their broad frames set with shining wood and tall windows. Below, sun glints off the lake. The valley's hills roll with green and gold.

It's hard to believe this is the same place where I arrived on that chilly January day. I'm glad I decided to stick around in Vernon after all. Springtime is in full bloom and there's so much more to this place that I still haven't seen.

At last, we pull up to a stop. "And you'll be home next Monday. In time for supper?"

"Wouldn't miss it." I open the door and hop down. My sneakers land on fresh, wet grass. Warm air runs across my face and I let out a long, slow breath.

Tracing familiar steps, I give Jean one final wave before ducking into the open garage door. Maggie's hunched over a portable keyboard, plucking out a tune. Pippa's at her side, scratching down a few notes onto a sheet of music. "Hey, buds." I wave. "How's practice going?"

"It'd be going a lot better if we had our lyrics ready." Maggie makes a long face. "We'll be in Kelowna in a couple of hours and we've gotta have something new for the show at Milkcrate."

"Rude." Pippa sticks out her tongue. "You can't rush art. Right, Lucien?"

"Oh, no." Maggie scowls at her partner. "Don't you go roping him into this."

"But maybe he can help," Pippa points out. Pushing up her glasses, she passes over some scribbled notes. "Can you take a look at it?"

"I don't want to mess with your process." They both whine and I laugh, stepping backwards into the house. "Fine, fine. I'll read it over in a bit, okay?"

As I pass through the kitchen, I find Camilla and Reg nestled in the breakfast nook. "Lucien, my boy."

Reg bristles his moustache into a smile. "Good to see you!"

Camilla sips her tea. "What's your mood scale for the day? Did you get some proper sleep?"

"I'll get back to you on that," I chuckle while perching on my toes to reach my usual mug. "Can I get some of that Earl Grey?"

"Of course." Camilla stirs a spoonful of honey into her cup and passes over the teapot. "Oh, and did you manage to book an appointment with that colleague of mine?"

"I did, actually." I pour and slowly take my first sip. It's perfectly steeped. "The first couple appointments have been really good."

"Oh, let the boy go see who he came here to see," says Reg, with a nod towards the hall. I give a wave of thanks and slip along the hardwood floor. My fingertips trace figure-eights along the wall. I stop at Alder's bedroom and peek through his cracked doorway.

Alder lies splayed on the bed, scrolling through his phone. When I knock, he glances up and beams.

"You made it!"

"Of course!" I set aside my tea and fall into bed beside him. "There's no way I'd miss this. Maggie and Pippa's first big show in Kelowna, then our flight to Toronto for your consult!"

"Totally perf." Alder flashes me his phone screen. "I was just looking up places to visit when we go out east. I want to do all the touristy stuff."

"Don't worry about all that," I tell him, pulling out my notebook. I scribble down a few thoughts as they slip through my mind. "My mothers already sent a list of places to take you. Plus, they've got the bedroom all set up. Jeanette found a new place after all."

"That's awesome!" Alder smiles a kiss against my forehead.

I lean against his chest and tap my pen on the page. "Can you think of a rhyme for *boyfriends*?" I ask. "All I have so far is 'joy trends.'"

"You're the poet," Alder chuckles. He lifts my chin to meet my eyes. "I can't wait to see the city with you. This is gonna be amazing."

"Well . . ." I let my notebook fall aside. "I, for one, can wait a little longer." He laughs, breath warm against my face. When we kiss, my body melts in his hands. I can feel his heartbeat, in sync with mine.

Acknowledgements

Thank you to many people who made this book possible. Firstly, Andrew. My partner, my love. Thank you for listening to my stories and nurturing my big ideas.

My grandparents: Bill and Cheryl, Tony and Heather. You have always believed in my capacity for storytelling. I am who I am, thanks to you.

My editor, Kat Mototsune, for all your guidance, patience and support. Thank you to you and all the people at Lorimer who helped this story find its way into the world.

My cousin, Alexa, and all my relatives out in Vernon: Thank you for the holiday dinners and walks in the forest. I am so glad to call you my family.

Michiko, for helping this story along every step of the way, including spending a hot, summer day live-reading the whole thing over video chat.

Finally, my dear friends (in no particular order): Hannah, Shane, Myriad, Lauren, Cea, Caitlin, Tamar and Jasbina. Thank you for distanced walks, yard hangs, zoom calls. I could never have made it this far without you.